Memories Cached

A Novel

Memories Cached

By Cameron Su

This novel is a work of fiction. Names and characters are the product of the author's imagination and any resemblance to actual persons, living or deceased, is entirely coincidental.

First published by Cameron Su in Hong Kong in 2017.

ISBN: 978-988-78568-1-8

This book is dedicated to the students everywhere who encounter the adverse effects of traditional and cyberbullying.

Foreword

Three years ago, I embarked on an effort to take a stand on bullying, a topic that has resonated with me as a teenager. Memories Cached seeks to document a striking and humorous tale regarding the teenage experience through various vantage points. Based upon semi-anecdotal situations and pure imagination, Memories Cached seeks to address two types of bullying: the time-tested traditional variety of physical and psychological bullying and the timeless one that Millennials face, cyberbullying.

The novel features dueling male and female narrators, in an unconventional protagonist versus antagonist scenario. The timeline highlights students transitioning from middle school to high school, all set in tropical Singapore. Ranked third in the world behind Latvia and New Zealand for bullying among 15-year-olds by an OECD study in 2015, the sovereign city-state could be replaced by any number of countries in the world for purposes of the plotline. According to the Programme for International Student Assessment (PISA), the Hong Kong Special Administrative Region ranks 16th while

South Korean students are reputed be the least bullied among the 50 nations surveyed.

As described by the PISA study and demonstrated in the novel, bullying can take on various forms, some of which are less than obvious:

- Physical (hitting, punching or kicking)
- Verbal (name-calling or mocking)
- Relational/social exclusion (or even more egregious public humiliation or shaming)
- Taking possessions belonging to another
- Cyberbullying (banter vs. outright bullying).

In some cases, there are instances where student safety issues arise well beyond circumstances pitting a bully against a victim.

In the preparation and finalization of the manuscript, I relied on the wise guidance and advice of many influential persons in my life. Special thanks go to Carolyn Nightingale, my eighth grade language arts teacher, who inspired me to write beyond the classroom; George Coombs, my ninth grade humanities teacher, who reviewed and commented on the manuscript; and New York Times best-selling author Da Chen, who mentored me.

The publication of this novel was achieved in part due to a grant by the Powered by Youth/Action for a Cause program sponsored by Kids4Kids in Hong Kong, a leading charity that addresses the myriad issues facing students. A portion of the proceeds of Memories Cached book sales will go toward a charitable donation to Kids4Kids. Further, in 2018-19, I will collaborate with Kids4Kids and child psychiatric professionals to discuss anti-bullying and mental health issues in the public and private schools of Hong Kong.

Writing Memories Cached has been a cathartic experience I'll never forget, an arduous process that has proved up my life experience thus far. I've dug through my life as a student, a friend and human being for the past three years, in search of experiences and ideas that would strike a chord with readers like yourself.

Cameron J. Su

Junior
Hong Kong International School
December 2017

CONTENTS

THE PRELIMINARIES

Chapter 1

A Series of Flashbacks | Circa Eighth Grade

The school bell heralds the end to a somewhat monotonous day. The five-second clanging lingers in my head. Students dash through the narrow door towards their lockers, causing a mini stampede.

Singapore's humidity remains hard at work again today, as always. The rolling thunder in the distance signals a possible thunderstorm. At least the storm might clear the haze caused by the burning forest fires in neighboring Sumatra and Borneo.

My buddy Archie straddles a small planter next to his locker, signaling me to huddle. Time for another strategy session. Not exactly a troublemaker, more of an instigator, Archie eggs on his friends into actions that no mother would condone.

It's the middle school years at Singapore International School. Seven hours a day of Language Arts (English and Putonghua), Science, Math, Social Studies and P.E. The same gig for all junior high schoolers worldwide, except for the additional dose of Putonghua. Spanish would be easier for those of us whose native tongue is English.

"Dominic, you know how this works," Archie smirks. "We discussed this last night on Skype, and you accepted the dare. It's only fair. You kiss your girlfriend, and I will ask out my crush."

I begrudgingly nod my head in agreement.

"The rules are simple," Archie stipulates. "The event must occur in a public space on school grounds. Timing is key. I'm sure you don't want others besides me to know about this. Classrooms and auditoriums are fine. Hallways and stairways work but closets and basements are off-limits."

Here we go again. I feel like I'm being blackmailed, or manipulated in some way. The more Archie glares at me, the more I'm skeptical. What is behind this cajoling?

But this had to be done. Is the timing right, not to mention the venue?

I skimmed the Student Handbook when I entered Middle School, but I would have guessed that Public

Displays of Affection were banned on campus.[1] Gosh, I recall signing a slip that recorded my agreement to the rules of being a Middle Schooler.

In reality, my love-interest, Talinda Chang, had also teased me in her TBH (To Be Honest) entries on Facebook:

> **TL: tbh, you're pretty nice and sweet. You're also a great friend and we have been through a lot in the past. throwback to the time when we were in the same class in fifth grade. don't even remind me when Mr. Palmer flipped your desk over when you were caught disrupting the class. haha. no one face-palmed when Palmer left the school at the end of the year for his OTT action. anyways, we should definitely hang out more!**

---

[1] Section 102 of the Singapore International School Student Handbook states:

It is important that students demonstrate an attitude and behavior regarding interpersonal relationships that would be acceptable to people of various cultural, ethnic and religious backgrounds. Students must refrain from inappropriate behavior such as intimate and prolonged embraces, kissing and similar actions that may be offensive to students, teachers, staff or to the general public.

Memories Cached

Underline the word: friend. Most of the comments in that TBH entry understated our true budding relationship, daring both of us.

Talinda had even tallied brownie points every time I did something an ordinary pubescent teenager would not do:

- lugging her books to Chinese class,
- carrying her lunch tray, and
- opening the door for her and her obnoxious crew.

I had reached the first-level 50 points just three days earlier—enough to secure a peck on the lips.

It would be my very first kiss. Oh, what have I gotten myself into?

Too bad I mentioned hitting the 50-point threshold to Archie.

I bolt from the second floor to the amphitheater as the immature brat continues to hound me from behind. For some odd reason, the kid's shoes are banging really loudly on the steps.

An unfamiliar teacher strolls past us, giving us somewhat suspicious looks. No after-school activities were scheduled in that part of the darkened school.

A lightning storm begins to brew in the near distance. Singapore leads the world in lightning strikes.

"Now's your chance . . . Whoops, sorry for announcing that too loud."

Oblivious, the teacher wanders right past, eyes again trained on her iPhone.

"That was close," Archie jokes.

I roll my eyes.

"Oh, look, there she is," Archie says, pointing at Talinda. I take a deep breath—the kind of breath wind instrument players need tackle a lengthy musical phrase—and then proceed down the stairwell.

After graduating from four square and wall ball after Upper Elementary, I rarely head down towards the open air amphitheater. Another reason is because Lower Elementary students invaded Middle School since the start of this school year as their original campus was torn down for redevelopment. Now, bicycles, scooters and even a luxurious playground occupy a large portion of the original amphitheater space.

As Talinda's eyes and mine lock, she shoots me a reluctant smile.

"Ya ready?" I ask Talinda as both of us go behind the pillar inside the amphitheater, preparing for the showdown. Hope it's not a letdown.

"Sure thing."

I walk towards Talinda and realize that both of us could tangle up with our braces. I was due to have my braces removed in a month. Perhaps we should hold off. Doc Lim gave me some wax to cover my braces during clarinet practice but I never tried it out. It would have come in handy now, though it's probably wilting in the fridge now.

Talinda appears not the least bit nervous. She must've done this before.

As it is new territory for me, I don't know what to do next. Reach out for her hand, or hands? Grab the back of her head? Should've asked Archie for advice. Not that he knows any better.

Not sure why I didn't balk but I just strode up to Talinda and just puckered up. It was a peck that only lasted a second or so. I think I tilted my head to the right. Can't recall exactly.

Talinda's lips and mine slowly drift away from each other as we unlock our lips. Bittersweet joy mix with awkwardness after the quick smooch. At least one of us were rookies at this kind of thing.

The only kisses I know come from watching comedies and romantic movies. Mom scolded Dad when he selected one of those Will Ferrell classics. Whenever a problematic scene appeared, one of them paused the DVD while the other summoned me to the adjoining bathroom. Little did they know that I would peek through the door, as any curious child would. Who are you to judge me?

Dad picks good flicks. Mom is humorless on this subject.

The rub is that I will have to re-sit for each of those movies when I'm 17 or so.

Thank goodness our braces do not clasp together.

"Was that okay with you?" I ask, clueless as to what Talinda had felt. Her eyes appear to sparkle. We are both unsure of what had just happened. Both of us experienced a sensation that is hard to describe. Not surprisingly, she utters not a single word in response.

She's a cool cat.

She about-faces and sprints away immediately towards the awaiting buses, without saying goodbye. I guess I didn't really need a goodbye.

A first kiss was just enough to make my day.

Or was it?

After what seemed like a long minute, I just stand behind the amphitheater, feet planted, all to myself. I couldn't take in the sequence of events that just occurred.

Yes, who would have the courage and the nerve to do such a thing at this innocent age? The audacity to make a girlfriend tag along after school towards the back of the amphitheater ever so secretly, and then unload a kiss? Isn't that so completely out of whack? Isn't that considered, to say the least, outrageous behavior? Not to mention contravening the Student Handbook for an egregious PDA?

Red card, go straight to jail.

Time out. Where was Archie during the past few minutes? Did he bolt for the buses after he saw that I was heading down the stairwell? Else, did he hover from the rafters, making sure that his dare was taken up? Either way, I wouldn't discover the truth, especially after asking the kid.

I check the ceiling and the walls to make sure that absolutely no CCTV recorded the escapade. "Good," I say to myself, calmly. I turn behind, and—

BAM!

I run headfirst into what I think was one of those tall, blue cushioned pillars in the amphitheater. What appears to be the assistant principal, Mr. Samuel Sadlowski, is just a monstrous obstacle blocking my escape.

I am planked on the ground (not in the cool way), half groggy, readying myself to chase down the afternoon school buses, until I run yet again into a perfectly stiff and sweaty arm.

Indeed, Mr. Sadlowski is a reality. It now appears that I am not going to catch my bus in time. Facing Mom's grimace for being home late and having to hail a taxi are now the least of my worries.

Give me a pencil and a few boring classes and you'll likely find some doodles on my textbooks rather than actual mental work. That's probably the basis of my study habits.

In fact, you could give me three nights' worth of homework and I still wouldn't touch it until the last minute.

My name's Savannah Dixon. I am currently an eighth grader and a rising senior in high school. I say this because it makes me feel a million times closer to college and out of parental control.

I am another one of those Facebook flamers who exaggerate our existence. Case in point:

"Student at": *I'll pick my parents' 1st Choice (university rather than my actual middle school).*

"Lives in": *I'll select some cool city in California, such as Los Angeles.*

"Works at": *Let's pick Google, Apple or anything Silicon Valley. Snapchat would be even better.*

Profile photo: *I'll pick one that portrays me in the best light—that is, an unblemished face—even if it is from years previous.*

Common theme: *make me relevant by sensationalizing.*

That is to say, independence—ahem, college—is a million light years away. I've gotten enough solid grades in every class to be called "a smart student" but not quite a nerd. However, I am mindful that my yesteryears were my heyday. Sixth grade used to be simple enough. I would just have to read a book to get a gold star or a pencil with my name on it.

Just getting through the rigors of eighth grade is an ordeal. Thinking about the next month of my academic coursework, not to mention the uncertainty of teenage social life, is strenuous enough.

And right now, all I'm thinking about is what time it is, and how many more minutes I have to sit in this desolate room doing asinine homework, and why December and Christmas break lasted about five minutes, and what I just observed half an hour ago after school ended.

I saw a couple kiss.

Yes, that's right. Under the school amphitheater. While all the cliques and the outsiders were wandering freely, gravitating to the buses and the school driveway where chauffeur-driven rich kids are picked up, a boy in a soccer jersey with pointy blue sneakers approached his girlfriend down there for a "smooch."

"Unreal," I thought at that precise moment, immediately taking out my smartphone for a quick video.

I suspected something was up as I saw two guys caucusing while a gal approached from the other stairwell.

I checked around to see if anyone had noticed the kissing. That pestering kid, Archie, after watching his wingman Dominic walk down the stairs to complete the deed, face-palmed himself as he whisked away from the tender scene.

I grimace at how Dominic hit on Talinda in the cafeteria just last week. Both reached for an orange drink carton simultaneously. Dominic withdrew quickly, trying to blink but only managed to move both eyes—one only slightly more than the other.

Much of the school was unaware an event in Singapore International School history was underway. Perhaps a story that could even make the headlines on social media, the Net in general and then shock the sovereign city-state. Then again, it would have been hilarious if the brace-faces interlinked metals with one another.

That didn't happen.

After that big moment, all I could remember was that I dashed for my life towards the buses, not leaving a single trace. And on the bus, my mind forever wandered as I fought hard to keep the secret to myself.

Chapter 2
Reality Crushed

I don't want to be here.

I sit in the assistant principal's office under an ominous cloud of immense guilt and uncertainty, waiting for my death sentence. I'm frozen, hunched back, praying for my release from this hellhole.

Don't forget I reside in Singapore, where drug mules and users get the death penalty. Chewing gum-riddled escalators resulted in an island-wide sales ban. Foreigners can pack gum for "personal use" but anything more would kick in a citizen's arrest.

I never wondered whether my school was organized under American principles (third strike and you're out) or the more draconian local variety.

The bruise on my forehead caused by hitting Mr. Sadlowski's forearm mimicked fresh pimples. I feel chubby; my cheeks, swollen.

My left ear, also swollen and inflamed, reminds me of how I ended up in this office, by way of a primitive method known as ear dragging. Wasn't this banned in the United States in the past century?

Mom used to say that the longer the ear lobes (We're Chinese), the longer the life, sort of like Buddha himself.

In my case, one of my ear lobes has been unceremoniously extended. I didn't even have to consult a plastic surgeon.

In an odd way, it would have been better if Mr. Sadlowski ear dragged both of my ears to balance things out.

Mr. Sadlowski always performs this ritual on the troublemakers as a way of cruel and unusual punishment. I don't suppose the Model UNers would be able to intervene. Perhaps that's why he intimidates everybody in the school, even other teachers. His 6-foot, 3-inch frame and somewhat menacing demeanor prove why many students choose to avoid him in the hallways.

No changes of direction but certainly emulating the parting of the Red Sea with students hugging the lockers and walls as Mr. Sadlowski parades down the corridors.

A few days back, Mr. Sadlowski caught the resident school bully, Ryan Chang, taunting Horace Han, the resident school nerd, in the cafeteria. The episode is forever engrained in my memory. Ryan threatened to launch rubbery meatballs at Horace using a spoon. Horace, who couldn't defend himself or hurt anyone but himself, cowered as a crowd gathered.

Memories Cached

"Horace! Horace! Horace!" some of the crowd (mostly boys) chanted in unison as Ryan catapulted meatballs at Horace's head. At each volley, Horace could only turn his head, not thinking of ducking below the table.

The cafeteria served lackluster Spaghetti Bolognese with Meatballs as the main entrée for the day. Poor Horace was just sitting there by himself, trying to stomach his spaghetti. The other entrée featured a vegetarian dish.

An errant meatball hit the back of Horace's head and then summarily dropped down the back of his white shirt, bleeding red sauce down his back. One of the final meatballs struck his head so hard that he accidentally swallowed one of the spaghetti strands down the wrong pipe.

As Ryan reared back for his final onslaught—this time with slimy, canned peaches—Mr. Sadlowski grabbed Ryan's wrist so hard that the kid dropped both the spoon and sticky peaches onto the back of his new Nikes.

Ryan grimaced; the gathering crowd gasped. Some wannabe hooligans cheered for a split sec.

Horace had no real reaction, except that of numbness. He only wondered whether he kept a spare set of clothes in his locker. He knew no one would offer up spare gym clothes for him to recover from the embarrassment.

Surely Sheriff Sadlowski would allow him to don gym clothes during school hours as an exception to the strict dress code regulations.

Mr. Sadlowski ear dragged Ryan two floors down towards the office, to many of the students' delight. Amazing how Long Lobe still made it through that day and through the rest of the year, considering how much grief and utter humiliation he inflicted upon everyone. Justice had been rightfully served.

One of the trademarks of teenagers, especially boys, is how quickly they can turncoat on the main actors. At the outset of Horace Han's bullying, a squadron of boys and wannabe gang members cheered on Long Lobe; whereas, within seconds of Sheriff Sadlowski's arrival, most of the crowd appeared empathetic to Horace.

Ryan still toyed with the idea of macking on girls after the incident, but no single attempt seemed to work out.

At one point, I began to feel a bit sorry for him. Until this episode, some of us thought that Ryan was a reformed kid; what made him seem transcendent to some of his peers only dragged him down towards being an outcast.

But then again, with his eye-watering record of two suspensions and an untold amount of detentions, I threw that idea out of the calculus. The only issue here is whether his current digression merits a suspension or a detention. Either way, he doesn't bother the school bus driver or bus mother for a few days, not to mention his fellow students.

Back to my predicament.

Ironically, Mr. Sadlowski acts as if he were the lead principal. Scratch that, he acts as if he were the head administrator of the entire school system. While all that may be true in his solitary mindset, to the community he is not.

He's taking ever so long to begin this discussion. As if I'm the prominent troublemaker in the school. By now, Long Lobe must be able to impersonate Mr. Sadlowski in a TedTalk regarding How to Exact Discipline upon Middle School Students.

That TedTalk would be a universal theme, applicable to school administrators and teachers worldwide. Ear-dragging aside, which would be forbidden Stateside, might be fair game in the emerging countries in Asia, Eastern Europe, countries in the former Soviet Union, South America and Africa. In short, the rest of the world.

But, hey, Singapore is reputed to be a first world country.

Long Lobe and Sadlowski hang together, albeit the former is forced to do so.

Sadlowski jabbers and flirts with his wife Andrea, the lead school secretary, who consistently sports outlandish garments from the late 70s. Today's pantsuit encompasses the entire color spectrum of a V8 juice can. Just the sight of this makes me want to puke.

I'm guessing their music of choice was disco (Donna Summer and early Michael Jackson) rather than hard rockers like Bon Jovi and Metallica.

The clock says 3:30 p.m.—an agonizing 20 minutes since school ended. Is Mr. Sadlowski purposely postponing this?

My homeroom teacher, Mr. Hensley, enters the neighboring canteen area and pours himself a glass of milk tea and glances over to my direction. I silently pray that he doesn't ask me any questions. We both exchange waves.

I seem to recall that I had a run-in with him before.

Mr. Sadlowski's clomping shoes reaches my earshot.

"And your name is?" Mr. Sadlowski queries in his heavy Polish accent. Someone said he's originally from Chicago—Polish Downtown, of course. It's a miracle that he doesn't know my name, as I'm a lifer at the school, starting first as a nursery school scholar. I think he even taught some math to my older sister, Erin, prior to his promotion to the dictatorship.

"Name's Chiu. Dominic Chiu," I say emphatically, resembling one of those British spymasters.

"That's nice, Dominic. Come on over to my office."

Mr. Sadlowski's office exemplifies his arrogant self. The lightly used chalkboard is scrubbed to a stark slate, reserving enough space for every possible ornament or decoration, including every single school-related announcement, even those from previous academic years. The unused chalks—tricolors of red, white and yellow—line the tray neatly next to the dust-free erasers.

An over-sized coffee machine sits cozily inside an unlatched closet shelf, next to other shelves that are filled generously with an assortment of folded dress shirts, suits and golf magazines.

Challenging word problems adorn the walls, confirming that he was once a math teacher. His S-shaped, black marble desk barricades all his paraphernalia.

"Welcome to the kingdom, Dominic. Take a seat. Make yourself cozy in one of these chairs," Mr. Sadlowski enunciates, wielding a half-chewed Snickers bar he started on earlier in the day. He wolfs down the last third and then tosses the wrapper into the wastebasket.

"You have an immaculate office," I offer. My father used to say that a clean desk is the sign of a sick mind. Hopefully, a bit of joking around would give me an opportunity to escape this as soon as possible. I had never been to the principal's office before. I decide to withhold the extra commentary.

I need to ask Dad what it means if a school administrator has an errant peanut fragment hanging on the left side of his month.

"They don't call me a prestigious, luxurious man for nothing," he snickers ostentatiously in that tiresome pseudo-Polish-American accent.

Oh, that accent, not to mention his off-putting personality.

And that wicked mint breath of his, now mixed with chocolate, nougat and nuts. All I want to do right now is to suck in air through my mouth to my diaphragm, exhaling as late as possible. To my dismay, my sinuses are not acting up.

"But let's get straight to the discussion, Dominic, as you invited trouble." He clears his throat and runs his right hand up a streak of sweaty, gelled hair.

"What, exactly, were you doing down there in the amphitheater?"

Quick, say something, speak the truth, I try to coach myself.

"What's that you say?"

"Um, nothing."

Mr. Sadlowski widens his bright blue eyes and glares at me. He probably thinks I did something really egregious even though I didn't.

Somehow, this is much worse than yelling. Oh, the agony.

Sheriff Sadlowski undoubtedly knew the answer to the question posed. No doubt he's like every other adult in my life.

"C'mon, don't be scared," he offers but does not relent. "You look like you want to say something."

"Look," I begin. Not a good word choice for an opener.

"My best friend Archie dared me to kiss a girl. He tried and tried to coax me into the idea, but I was very doubtful. Eventually, the situation got to the best of me, and I had no other choice but to kiss her."

"You . . . kissed . . . a girl?" Mr. Sadlowski mockingly restates as he works a toothpick to pick out the extraneous nuts. The toothpick is the hardcore, industrial kind that looks like a mini sword (plastic rather than wooden, with a tiny floss string that buckles on first insertion). Useless, in other words.

"Yes, I did, in fact."

Pause.

I suddenly realize that Mr. Sadlowski might not have seen the kiss. He didn't even ask me to name my co-conspirator. Shoot. Did coming clean work to my disadvantage?

Perhaps I should have just said that I was hanging out in the amphitheater with my GF, just to chat. What have I done?

Mr. Sadlowski's face turns beet purple after holding his breath for an inordinate amount of time. He laughs scornfully, banging his propped-up shoes on his desk and mocking me. Oh no, he's just loosened his loafers by each alternate foot. Bad breath is one thing.

He is unable to contain himself, dropping his shoes onto the floor and rocking uncontrollably in his swivel chair.

I will not be able to pick him off the floor, assuming I could even muster a single, full breath in the coming minutes.

Never have I ever witnessed that much laughter in a school administrator or teacher of any sort. Strike that, no adult except when my Dad and I watched those Will Ferrell flicks.

Clumps of melted chocolate cluster on the edges of his mouth, not to mention that errant peanut that escaped the tooth prodder.

He wipes his lips with his sleeve and contemplates, finally reverting to a solemn state. By this time, Mrs. Sadlowski has perked up next door and wonders whether this episode involves punishment or a superlative inside joke.

"Well, Dominic, here's the ironic part."

"What's that?"

"This is the first occurrence of a breach of the PDA rule in the 40-year history of Singapore International School. Congratulations. You've just made school history."

Wait, PDA? Then I remember—the amphitheater wasn't entirely barricaded. Dang it!

During the past day, I have been a less than conscientious student, perhaps more devious than normal. My Language Arts teacher, Mrs. Harper lambasted me when she discovered I was surfing the web.

"Off task" is what the teachers like to say. "Works efficiently and uses time productively in class" comprises the third section of the often-feared "Work Habits" checklist that prevents some of the brightest students, especially the math geniuses, of their honors award at the end of each semester.

Great aptitude, lousy attitude.

But in my estimation, being off task is the direct result of a teacher lacking the ability to captivate each and every student in engaging lessons.

Two types of teachers abound at the school. The first variety tend to hand out instruction-based assignments rather than lecturing. Forget about asking questions via the Socratic method. The second variety favor the chalkboard and/or overhead projector. Math teachers are relegated to this method as they demonstrate problem-solving and equations step-by-step.

Unbeknownst to the couple, I was stalking them—just a bit. I remember being forced to sit in the corner in Language Arts class after browsing through a past yearbook when I was supposed to be reading "Of Mice and Men." Unfortunately, I was able to discover the boy's identity, but not the girl's.

"Dominic Chiu," I reminisced the name and the picture. My, oh my, what a cheeky face with cute dimples. I must have looked at the yearbook published in the previous decade because that Dominic is not the growth-spurted, stud I saw a day ago. Mushroom hair, thin

eyebrows, a teddy-bear style nose and a small mouth were his most prominent features back in the day.

Pity that Dominic is now forced to face the wrath of Mr. Sadlowski. My last recollection of Sheriff Sadlowski involved him reprimanding Ryan Chang for tossing meatballs in the school cafeteria. He had a field day against that powerless Horace Han.

As pitiful as Horace seemed on that fateful day, I now realize that I held a potential weapon even more powerful than the never-ending taunts of a school bully.

My, look what my world has come to.

Chapter 3

The So-Called "Flawless Résumé"

Oh, did I mention I forgot to tell Mom and Dad about the earlier incident? They always tell me it is better to reveal any mistakes earlier than later. Mom will roar and immediately tell Dad if she discovers I hid the truth for just two or more days.

By not confiding in them immediately after a misdeed means I have lied. Both parents can sense something's up when I mutter one-word responses to the question: "How was school?"

Because they forbid me to kiss any girl, much less date girls, I know they will be mad at me regardless if I mention the issue immediately or not. This is perhaps my greatest psychological issue. I spend most of my time ruminating over my choices rather than committing to one like a man.

What a dilemma. I'm not old enough to facilitate my own decisions, yet I'm not young enough to be deemed innocent.

I bet many young teens can relate to this.

To the contrary, it was a conscious decision not to confide. As that thought is now stuck in my head, my mind thrusts into overdrive. What happened to the trustworthy, honest Dominic?

The scary thing is, school is like a coming of age movie, such as that Academy-Award winning epic, "Boyhood." That thing took a long 12 years to film. The irony is, it took me only a couple of years in middle school to get my first kiss.

Any parent would say teenagers are maturing too quickly. I second that. In the 21st century, it's a reality. Teens are bound to evolve over time.

I'll give an example. Puberty, hormones out of whack. Teenage rebellion. Talking back. Teens acting out. Experimentation. First kiss. What does love have to do with anything?

What is love?

What gives?

Are there any second chances?

It's called puppy love—a very shallow thing that hardly ever lasts. Or is this just an infatuation?

I can't bear the thought of going to school with the possibility of being mocked by my friends and teachers. What would happen to my reputation? What would happen to my flawless résumé of outstanding marks in every single subject?

Mom now echoes: What would happen to your achievements in school? She actually means "our" as she tutors me in math and Chinese.

Whoa. I hope Mom didn't actually say that. Moms say what they think; they think a lot.

Once again, I wake up 10 minutes before the 6 a.m. alarm sounds. Too early to get up and wash up and much too late to get back to sleep. To wake up a millisecond before the alarm sounds is cool but this circumstance isn't. I must have awoken from the tail end of a nightmare.

Was that résumé commentary from Mom part of that dream? It was re-iterated incessantly—surely mindless echolalia is not indicated.

"DOM-in-ic! Wakey-wakey," Mom yells. "Time to wake up!" And then she says the same thing again, this time in Putonghua.

Good. She's just calling me over to breakfast.

I walk out of my bedroom, morose and sulky. Pondering on this topic has deprived me of nearly three hours of deep sleep.

All the notorious gamers who get off task in school sleep very late at night and oversleep the next morning, often tardy for their first period.

I will join them in collective yawning today.

Memories Cached

I saunter into the breakfast nook in the kitchen. Erin, my older sister, has just polished off her breakfast, which usually consists of a light pastry and orange juice. "The prelude to another one of her outrageous school days," she often quotes.

She ties up her laces on her khaki boots, then catwalks out the front door towards the bus stop with a smug look on her face. Twenty minutes early and half awake, Erin is desperate to chat with her boyfriend.

I know exactly what that smug look means.

It means that I'm relegated to sitting at the table alone with Mom. Having worked late, Dad is snoring away in a bedroom several rooms down the hallway. Dad's snore gene is inherited through his father. It's not the gurgling type, just the simple crescendo of a cyclone—repeating incessantly until he decides to sleep on his side, or just wake up.

Mom and Erin tell me that I also snore, with a sound that mimics rice porridge reaching the boiling point—the chugging and gurgling variety.

I got Dad's gene. It's the Chiu gene.

Now, I have to face the awkwardness of Mom's persistent questioning. A most irritating time of the day that even our dog, a mixed breed collie, Pudgy hates.

Yes, Mom, I know. You're giving me that smug glare resembling that of Erin's. You're going to ask me a gazillion more questions about what I'm currently studying, which people I have recently made friends with, if I have a girlfriend, if I had gotten into trouble, or why my face is looking the complete opposite of yours.

If I offer that I have excelled in something, you will inevitably say that I can do better. If I offer that I need some help in some coursework, you will break out the scrap paper to re-teach what I already know or worse yet, teach me something I don't need to know.

I'll have to give it to her. If I ever win an academic award and need to thank my peeps, I'll first mention Mom. She's the one who knows my coursework better than my teachers, almost as if she were attending school all over again.

Mom's forté is math and Putonghua. Like in Mainland China, the Chinese taught in Singapore is based upon the simplified characters, as opposed to the traditional characters used in Hong Kong and Taiwan.

I can read the comics.

Dad's strength is in history, science that does not involve high math (biology and chemistry but not biochemistry) and English.

Great, I've got Tiger parents that cover most subjects.

Wow, that was my ongoing train of thought.

Now for Mom's daily breakfast: raisin bran with a smattering of fresh fruit.

"Mom, can you make the bagels they make in Panera Bread?" I ask. I often reminisce about our summer vacations Stateside. "You know, the Steak and Egg? I think that will suit my palate a bit better," I query, appearing frustrated with Mom's lack of originality. But really, I'm just stalling.

I admit I'm a bit foolish at times.

"Dominic, you'll remember years ago that I used to feed you and your sister bagels for breakfast. I later read that pre-packaged bagels are too processed and unhealthy," she responds.

I don't quite remember. I was so young that every single food out there tasted the same.

Except wasabi.

I mean, that thing can kill. Call it literally: "green inferno."

Speaking of fires, I'm feeling one crackling in my eyes. Sooner or later, there's going to be a deluge of tears down my face, full throttle.

Real men don't cry. I haven't cried in eight years since I tripped off my skateboard, dislodging my baby front tooth. Just like how I've never puked in my life—I don't know if it's good genes or just a miracle. I suppose one good thing is that I don't suffer from vertigo, sea- or airsickness and don't necessarily need to sit in the front seat of a car in motion.

That said, I came close to puking the other day when Snicker remnants surrounded Mr. Sadlowski's mouth.

Snickerdoodoo.

Luckily, Mom can't tell why I released an errant tear from my left eye. In her mind, she's swapping between what's on tap for dinner, given the breakfast discussion, or something else.

Perhaps she knows I'm not telling the truth, and hides that to trick me into lying even more. Like many of my troublemaking friends, Mom enjoys luring me into lying. Weird, am I right?

She's ready to pounce on her prey.

"Something's just on my mind, Mom."

She places her hand on my shoulder and nudges away my breakfast plate: "What's wrong, Dominic?"

Saying the truth now is inevitable. It just has to be done.

So I thought. As with the earlier encounter with Sheriff Sadlowski, coming clean actually worked to my disadvantage. I don't know if it'll work here or not. It's probably the better option.

Not to mention I haven't admitted to Mom that I got in trouble with the assistant principal.

Somebody, help a poor boy out.

"Uh, just a stupid biology project that I'm having trouble with, nothing much."

Good job, Dom.

I was learning chemistry in science class, not biology. For some odd reason, my lame excuse did not register with my ever-so insightful and probing Mother.

"Hmm. That's odd. I thought you were great at science and you could handle your own problems with all these projects," Mom responds, smiling. "It's okay, whenever you need help, Mommy's here. Daddy is here as well." She diverts her attention back to watching her Korean TV drama series.

That's how aloof Mom is being (or pretending to be) right now. It's kind of uncanny.

What's the deal with Korean TV? Or K-Pop in general? Last year, Mom focused on a series that featured a chef, not a counterpart to Gordon Ramsay in a modern Korean kitchen. Rather, that series was set in a Korean imperial palace of sorts. Sure, conspiracies can take place in any context, during any era. Next month she will be entranced by a TV drama set in a law firm in Seoul. Hey, I thought I was bound for med school.

Surprise, surprise. Mom let me off quite easily. Without further chitchat, I munch on my raisin bran promptly, then pack my bags and depart. Mom ventures off to the other side of the kitchen, preparing Dad's breakfast.

It isn't easy trying to escape the house discreetly. I say goodbye to Mom in the most reserved way possible.

She waves back. Yes. All is well. At least for now.

I lust for independence, away from the watchful eyes of my helicopter parents. That said, though I'm looking forward to my freedom in college, it will require quite a bit of discipline, which I lack. Opting for clarinet tutoring instead of Cub Scouts, I don't know how to pitch a tent or even more mundane, how to start the washing machine.

Dad says I made a big mistake avoiding Cub Scouts. Mom says Dad made a mistake enrolling me into an American school in my primary school days. If I had attended a local school earlier, then my Putonghua proficiency would have improved and Mom would be able to do less tutoring now.

Memories Cached

I remember Mom saying: "Thinking about college can wait. Just focus on each year, one by one." She's stated that repeatedly, oblivious to my whining. Of course, I continued to fight my constant urge to hurl bagels across the table. Pudgy would be keen on that result.

She even made kind of a flow chart in perfectly impeccable cursive writing, demonstrating her rules of life:

- No pencil = No written assignment accomplished
- No written assignment accomplished = No chance of passing the test
- No chance of passing the test = Failing the test
- Failing the test = Messy grade on report card
- Messy grade on report card = No chance to get into a good college
- No chance to get into a good college = No job
- No job = No girlfriend
- Girlfriend(s) possible = Make a few million first (major currencies only).

Think she got that off some BuzzFeed page. Mom is obviously a bit repetitive. Her expertise is emphasis mixed with hyperbole. She confuses alliteration with repetition of "No."

The tires on the bus screech to a complete stop at our neighborhood. The front left wheel goes up on the pavement curb; nobody knows if it was either intentional or a miscalculated blunder.

"Chi Sin!" the bus driver (akin to an agro "Geez" or something like that in one of the equivalent local Chinese dialects, Cantonese). The arriving students can hear the sound waves emanating the side window of the bus as his crackly voice provides a command performance; he was not assigned a new bus this year and rightly so. That's the window where he taps the ashes from his cigarette during his breaks. No culpability as the dash cam only records erratic driving.

He frowns in disgust and honks incessantly, the horn somehow as decrepit as his driving techniques.

Monday frowns are inevitable. Almost every student and parent has it. The sentiment is also inherent in the greeting teachers, who are there only by assignment and not volunteering. They share that common grimace.

Though inanimate, even that dilapidated bus has it.

Most of us can't even get up in the morning at 6 a.m. sharp without looking drowsy. For me, the common indicators are bags under my eyes, a crooked mouth and worse, one fresh pimple strategically located on the tip of my nose. I first got that one on Christmas Eve and it seems to reappear every four months or so.

Riley Smith, however, is immune to Monday blues. Upbeat Riley approaches me at the bus stop with an intimidating smile planted on his face. He's like that to everyone, no joke.

"Hey there, Dominos," he provokes. Few people are kind enough to greet me by my actual name. But this is strangely different.

Hmm. Maybe "kind" isn't the most suitable term for this situation.

"What's the haps, man?" I reply rather sarcastically. It's the phrase I usually use when chatting Archie on Skype, followed by short sections of casually bad grammar and the occasional profanity.

By chance, if Archie ever screenshots our embarrassing online conversations and posts it on my Facebook wall on my birthday, I threaten to dump the whole pepper shaker in his soup noodles the next day.

This is our bro code, and this is why we are such close friends.

"Everything's going good," Riley says. "And yourself?"

"Everything's cool, yeah." We head onto the bus. Riley kind of cuts in line flamboyantly as I step onto the first step, resulting in a rather awkward situation.

"Um, dude?" Both of us are squished in between the bus doorway.

Five seconds in, Tammy Moodley says: "You're causing a massive disturbance in the line, you two."

I turn to look at the line behind us, each person characterized with the exact frowning faces. It couldn't have been orchestrated better in Bollywood.

Madame Tang, the bus mother, has yet to intervene. She's always ready to pounce. The last thing I need is to be written up due to Smiley Riley causing this commotion.

"It's really not my fault," I complain. "It's this guy over here." I try to elbow Riley but only more uncomfortable friction escalates. I'm at a loss, thinking that this could cause another unfortunate event.

"Why don't you just squeeze out and try again?" I eke out. Perplexed and not heeding my rational advice, he charges forward full speed up the bus and into the back row, and then lies down across the empty five seats.

That pompous boy is as obnoxious than ever.

I want to take a seat the farthest from Riley. Then again, I want to be furthest away from the bus mother who exudes the traits of a tyrant. The halfway mark of the bus would be the best spot.

Nice. I'm right next to the primary schoolers, at least one of whom always balls her eyes out when her mother waves goodbye.

"Hurry up, you lazy hooligans! We will be late! We don't have enough time!" she says, almost recklessly shuffling some of the slow kindergarteners onto the bus. What she really wants to say is that she needs to get to her dim sum joint ASAP.

No mercy exists for those spacing out while in line. Especially the other Smith, Rusty, an anti-social fifth grader who looks like a panda sporting glasses. He has the exact opposite personality of Riley and has the density of an atom's nucleus. Yup, you heard me. A nucleus, approximated at: 2.3×10^{17} kg/m^3.

Maybe that was a bit of an exaggeration, but man, that kid is small AND densely stocky. That's probably why Riley turns a blind eye to him almost all the time. Not to be judgmental, but both of the Smith's personalities are grossly inverse.

After all, Riley is the president of our eighth grade class, which means he's favored by most people. In the seventh grade superlative section in the school's yearbook, he was named: "Future World Leader."

Cringe.

Out of curiosity, I turn back to check on the back row of the bus. Riley flips his narcissist, 16-year-old Bieber-hair, smiling at his own face on his iPhone's camera app. His gel formula somehow doesn't dissipate even after school's out. He's preparing for the chicks. Or aiming to be a teacher's pet. I'll never know.

I grab my noise-cancelling headphones from my backpack and place it on my head with certainty. I want to block out gradually the noises from the bus mother and the "pandamonium" caused by the chewing sounds of Rusty, the Human Panda. He chows down on this breakfast bun when Madame Tang isn't looking.

One of Rush's signature songs, "Tom Sawyer" appears on shuffle. Yeah, the Canadian rock band from Dad's teenage years. Classic rock with challenging time signatures.

I have this system where a randomly selected song from my iPhone determines my mood for the day. Sure, a bit superstitious. When hearing this song, the character Tom Sawyer from the book "Huckleberry Finn" comes to mind.

I reminisce those Tom Sawyer and Huck Finn days in third grade when I used to be another Asian juvenile delinquent in the school. The only test I ever aced in that grade was my eye test, with perfect 20/20 results. Grades didn't matter then as all the teachers had to assess was whether a student's work was satisfactory or unsatisfactory.

Whew. I try to digest all the events that happened thus far. I shut my eyes and my head droops, my forehead resting perfectly on the seat in front. The little guy in front is unbothered as he's too small to sit fully against the seat.

The second hand on the grandfather clock tempts midnight. Trivia pursued: It's been 33 hours following the couple's smooch. Amazing how I got this far in comparison with my otherwise boring life.

My sisters and the maids are asleep. And in the afternoon, Mom and Dad are off to Rangoon, Myanmar for charity purposes. They've arrived back at 12:30 a.m. from Los Angeles after a red-eye flight. Hardcore.

They have been dedicating most of her spare time to the local church, at the behest of the pastor. Their other hobbies include dabbling in philosophical books, especially those written by their favored philosopher: interestingly, Confucius. I suppose that's why we landed in Singapore, nicknamed Asia for Americans. Both highly regard associating with other people, especially those who are disenfranchised.

Unlike Dad, Mom abhors technology, sporting a ridiculously ancient flip phone. I think it was hand-made and the first to feature touch screens. But the battery life is good and that's all that matters, she remarks.

I'm in bed, watching the recorded video ad nauseam despite the poor quality. While eating cherries and spitting seeds out at the same time, I'm watching the video for the 58th time. It hasn't been uploaded but I can count to 58 without having to do a tally on paper.

I imagine people are going to break the replay button as I am doing right now.

I'm such a rascal, unlike my charitable, happy-go-lucky parents.

Now why have I not confided in my parents? Myanmar has mobile phone coverage, albeit spotty. I could raise the issue with them the following day—most likely in the afternoon after school, as they will probably sleep in until noontime.

I suppose this goes back to their hands-off policy of parenting. Unless the school counsellor or Mr. Sadlowski summons them to school, all is good. Frankly, even if I did want to consult with someone, I have no one to turn to—inside or outside my immediate family, or elsewhere.

In any case, the video is time-dated. Armed with precious footage of this variety, I might as well delete it unless I upload it within hours. That's the dilemma, as well as the attraction.

Honestly, I'm about to crash. Crash and burn, I should say.

But not before I post this video on YouTube and share the link with the entire school.

No, that would be too much. What if I get the couple into trouble— big trouble?

Doing so would be unprecedented in my relatively short life experience.

How about just sharing it with my classmates through WhatsApp? By the way, my parents prohibited me from using Snapchat, thinking the app was unsafe for pre-teens and teenagers. That app would have been the perfect medium.

It's too bad that I can't access the App Store without my father's password.

I suppose I could recruit somebody who has Snapchat but that would only delay the process, not to mention complicate it. I treasure my anonymity.

Wait, what do I care about the potential consequences? I'm not a friend—actual or online—with Dominic or Talinda. Nor do I have any intention of befriending either of them. Archie's an oddball.

But if I share the video, I might be called a hero to the community on the Net. The video might go viral. No clickbait at all.

Click. Click. Click.

Boom.

Gone.

In an instant, the seconds-long video is uploaded directly on YouTube and sent directly to my subscriber classmates and the world at large.

Should I also upload it to Stomp, Singapore's tattletale website where non-PC behavior gets written up in the relentless discourse of social media? Trollers would have a field day.

Then again, YouTube is international, big time.

Good night, Singapore.

Chapter 4
Underworld

My ears are fully focused on my iTunes playlist. My noise-cancelling headphones are doing their job. I'm drowning out the noise from the outside world.

But my eyes are wide open. My peripheral vision notices a couple of dudes looking at me funny. A gaggling group of six girls in front of me even stop to look behind—oddly all in perfect sync.

I sense that at least a dozen kids whisper my name—Dominic, Dominos (pizza chain), Dominoes (table game), Dom, Chiu dude, Chiu kid, etc. Most of them are peeps in my grade. Two are from the sixth grade. I'm not a fan of the sixth graders.

That's not good.

Ever-agile Archie comes from behind me and smacks my back with a solid forehand, causing me to lunge forward abruptly. "Ay, my mate." He's from Down Under today.

"Hey," I say, with a small grin.

"Unlike the British boys, you're a little milksop who doesn't have the guts to drink coffee for breakfast, so I'm giving you a caffeine boost for today. Who needs ginseng energy tonics? I saw your head drooping down, daydreaming or something. So you can thank me for boosting your spirits up a bit," he replies.

"Dude, do your parents know you indulge in caffeine highs at your tender age?" It's this type of sarcastic chitchat that keeps our friendship on good terms—almost parroting a poorly scripted dialogue from a Super Bowl commercial.

I'm in a rut. I have the thought of Talinda in my head, but I also carry the burden of that run-in with Mr. Sadlowski.

"You know, besides me spectating the other day, I think there was this other girl who was in the audience, too. The new couple really held court. Did you hear me applaud? You two are in. I was waiting for an encore."

"Well, yeah, no encore. And thanks a bunch for getting me into trouble. Deep trouble."

"What? I got you into trouble?" He's incredulous.

"Definitely. With Mr. Sadlowski. By the way, why did you take off right after the kiss? What's up with that?"

Archie raises his eyebrows. "Whoa, my bad. I really had to catch my bus as my mother grilled me last week for missing the bus once. Or was that twice? Never mind. That must've been pretty awful confronting him."

"Oh, you don't know that guy, man. Lemme tell you, it wasn't a good scene."

Both of us chortle.

"So who was that other girl spectating alongside you?"

"Oh, um. You know the girl who always dons the school's hooded jacket every day to keep her face obscure? Weird gal, especially taking into account how hot Singapore is in the summer. I mean, year-round."

"Give me some more detail, man. They all look the same," I joke. It's true; they do.

"Um, she wears red shorts most every day."

"And?"

"That's all I got. To be honest, I don't really know her name, though she's definitely in our grade. If you'd like, I can snipe her out easily."

"Nah, that's weird."

For a brief moment, I see a girl who looks exactly the same as the mysterious person I glanced at the other day—the one we were just talking about.

I spot Talinda, strolling across the school lawn alone, with none of her usual crew beside her. She seems rather depressed, which is the antithesis of her usual self. I realize I haven't talked to her in a while, which is a bit unusual for me. Usually, we would discuss our everyday lives, sometimes in person but most often through texting:

Chat with Talinda Chang on August 28, 11:25 PM

Me: heyy

Tal: heyo

Me: wassup

Tal: nothing much. u?

Me: so where do I stand?

Tal: 42 points and counting

Me: I thought I topped 45—didn't i close your locker?

Tal: 3 points deducted. u failed to lock it :/

Me: my bad. one step forward, two steps in reverse. :P

Tal: u can make it up later

Me: can't wait

Tal: c u

Me: adios!

I haven't taken Spanish as my Mom insists I continue Putonghua classes. Imagine a Chinese adult who can't speak his mother tongue properly, so Mom insists.

Dad, who spent a couple of years in Southern California, likes to dabble in a few handy Spanish words. I picked up "adios" and "amigos" from him. That's about it.

I leave Archie and dash across that lawn to confront Talinda.

Archie shakes his head at my impetuous move. Then he reconsiders by saying: "Go get'em."

The burden rests on me to regroup with her. For some odd reason, approaching her was a most nerve-racking experience. Texting would not suffice here.

Forget face-to-face face-offs.

"Talinda!" I yelp. I neither witness nor hear a response despite being within earshot from her. She does not even flinch.

With her permed hair unexpectedly frizz, she instead returns my greeting with a black face.

"What's wrong?" I question, stupefied and helpless by her outrageous expression. She was clearly hiding some kind of issue, possibly something insidious.

"Nothing," her mouth barely moves.

"I know there's something wrong, Talinda. This isn't you. We haven't talked since that afternoon and we need to catch up." The words seem to bite back as I say it. Kind of like a vocal migraine.

It was true. My mind was solely focused on staying away from trouble on the upcoming Summit school trip that I didn't really give much thought to Tal. I guess this issue is coming back to bite me. Something's amiss.

Her eyes are set on fast blink, and it's hard for me to tell whether she's trying to unload something on me.

In an attempt to decipher what is actually going on, I edge closer to her.

"Don't come closer," she replies, shoving a hand in my face, as if I popped her personal "bubble." Whoops.

Archie is still standing on that podium. He goes full-fledged pre-puberty, unleashing his signature megaphone-loud howl. In an odd way, Archie is genius when it comes to the opposite sex. He can decipher from body language when the guy has been shut down. Way down.

His voice cracks in a most irritating way.

"Get over here! We're already two minutes late for class. We're looking at demerits if we don't roll now."

At that point, I totally give up talking to Talinda. She isn't worth my time right now. I don't even say goodbye. I just turn towards Archie and take off.

The "voice crack" system is just another way of interpreting the odd friendship between Archie and myself. Archie purposefully exaggerates the voice cracking to irritate me as well as anyone around us. I'm not in the mood right now, though.

"Hey, Big Dom, watch out, we've got a new commando coming down the hallway. Woohoo!" Archie's voice is ever cracking.

In front of us, we spot a typical substitute teacher, just another anonymous person down the hall. She could even be a high school teacher. Who knows? Who cares?

She nears us. Good golly.

"This sort of behavior shall not be tolerated within this school premises," she blurts, her bottom lip protruding rather annoyingly followed by a menacing scowl.

Archie nods his head like one of those head-bobber toys at a local toy store or that commercial featuring NBA stars. Archie being Archie, he's overthinking things, sweating bullets profusely. He gets into lots of minor but embarrassing predicaments.

The teacher sashays away, high heels clicking rhythmically.

"You need a towel?" I murmur.

"Dominic, I was so scared!" Archie whispers sharply. "That woman had the eyes of a hawk."

"You should have seen your eyes. You were fast-blinking, super nervously." I stomp on Archie's foot.

"ARGH!" he screeches. "Dude, what was that for?"

"Didn't see you wearing sandals today. So much for dress code."

"Hey, can't you see the proctor right behind me?" Archie's soccer ball-sized head is blocking the view behind him. I glance over his shoulder. What looks like a miniature speck is that haunting face. The woman is staring us down, eyeballs disproportionately big. Bug-eyed.

Thankfully, homeroom is just a floor down from here. I dash as fast as I can down the stairs to avoid falling into this unnecessary situation.

Archie runs behind me, trying to catch up. "Quick, you fool! Move! She's gonna hunt us down!"

We both bolt, totally oblivious as to whether that teacher is chasing us now. We hope she isn't. Mr. Hensley, my math and homeroom teacher, is going to be pretty darn mad at me for being late for the eighth time this semester. Out of all my teachers, only Mr. Hensley is this precise in marking tardies.

Other teachers are sometimes tardy themselves. Tardies only pertain to students, though.

I enter homeroom, which is Room in 113. I take a deep breath, lugging on the door handle.

Giggles ripple all across the room, smirks on every student's face. I can hear jeers and smirks. There must be some other undercurrent going on. They're probably not laughing at my eighth tardy.

Mr. Hensley has an otherwise opposite expression; he is baffled. He perks up his glasses.

"Why—Dominic Chee-Yu—are you late, once again?" he enunciates irritatingly. His sound waves obliterate the ambient laughing of the class. Thank goodness he doesn't know my given Chinese name, as he would butcher it.

"Nothing, the bus arrived late due to heavy traffic," I gulp.

"Dominic, you've overplayed that excuse for the past five times. Can't you come up with something original?

"I really don't know. The bus driver is a bit of a dum-dum." I immediately regret saying that.

The whole class cracks up. Chad Wembley, the loudest and the most obnoxious kid in my homeroom, guffaws. His face motions mimic a fast-playing GIF file.

On Facebook, he's the kind of kid who would offer up a roast on someone else's pic just for the likes, and spend the entire next day thinking about it. One of his savage comments on someone's new profile pic amassed 55 "haha" reacts. In real life, I'm sure he means well.

Ed Cho, the Korean would-be mathematician, casts his eyes super wide and then face-palms on my behalf. Natalie Li almost falls out of her seat laughing. One kid in the back does semaphore, almost as if his crossed-arms signals would prevent me from using the standby excuse. I didn't mean to crack up the class but it worked to that effect.

Truth is, the entire class is dead set on prolonging the interruption to delay Mr. Hensley from his repetitive lectures on dress code, fire alarms and the like.

Mr. Hensley sucks in his potbelly and regurgitates a mouthful of incomprehensible words from his sesquipedalian dictionary, then says sternly, yet sarcastically: "That's funny, Dominic, but you'll have to stay after class for a discussion."

"Okay."

My classmates crowd their way out of the door to their first elective class, hissing and snickering away, especially the nerdy gamers in class.

Tess Chase, possibly the only female gamer in the eighth grade, just used her mother's credit card to purchase a new character in League of Legends. Despite staying up late every night gaming, she somehow has perfect attendance and is clockwork when it comes to arriving on time.

The noise levels gradually muffle, and eventually lessen to an awkward silence. Mr. Hensley rests a sweaty right palm on his desk, glaring at me with our eyes parallel to each other. "I'm going to ask you one more time, Mr. Chiu," he says.

"Mr. Hensley, there's no other way to explain it. The bus was stuck in traffic. It is what it is." That last line is oft repeated by adults but a no-go area for students. My bad. Oopsies.

I should have said something along the lines of "these were circumstances beyond anyone's control."

Mr. Hensley pauses for a bit, then ruminates, glancing at his desk, then back at me. Then, he unlatches his binder and opens it carefully to the class attendance page, scrutinizing each and every instance whereby I was late to homeroom. "Demerits," he says. He disregards the fact that I might be late to my next class right now. That would excavate me into even deeper trouble. I can't even ask for a late slip. What is this?

"Dominic, you can leave," he says, shooing me away. I trudge out the classroom door, looking all dispirited. My next class is four floors up. Elevators are off-limits for students during school time. In my mind, I curl back into my usual self.

As I walk solo, I think to myself, yeah, what's the point of homeroom anyway? High schoolers go straight to their first class. Middle schoolers head for a 10-minute homeroom gathering so that teachers can take attendance and send kids for detention following successive late arrivals. Noice.

I'd just like to mention that the 10-minute homeroom session should be dropped in favor of a 10-minute buffer for the first elective class. Good idea. That suits people like me.

Mindful that Creative Writing begins in approximately four minutes, I zoom towards the bathroom, pleading for a temporary refuge from the melodrama outside. I know Dominic is now subject to extreme ridicule, the kind for which teenagers can only exact. Regardless of his craziness and lack of judgment the other day, I was the one who made the episode viral.

I am not only the initiator, but also the arbiter of Dominic's, not to mention, Talinda's fate. This innate power overwhelms me.

Mr. Sadlowski's punishment, whatever form it might take, pales in comparison to my indiscreet use of the video to the detriment of Dominic and Talinda.

Even if I second guess my decision to upload, I can't really take it back. Even if I were to delete the upload, almost the entire student body has viewed the video. How do you erase human memory?

You kind of can't.

No doubt there will be at least one geek student well versed in copying videos on a surreptitious basis. Many "YouTube to MP4" conversion sites dominate the worldwide web. There's always that one guy who downloads the file before I have a chance to delete it. You don't even have to be a geek to complete this simple task.

Memories Cached

I punch the walls of the bathroom stall and hold the pose tightly. This is my shelter from the real world. The day thus far has been too overwhelming. I try to calm myself and settle down, reliving each episode, beginning with the first.

This morning, I missed the school bus.

I asked the old man Marcel Higgins across the street if he had seen the bus whisk by. Not pleased with his gardener's handiwork, Mr. Higgins re-mowed his front lawn, which is more manicured than the cow grass on the nearby golf course. He's an avid golfer who enjoys hitting hollow, plastic golf balls off that tightly mowed, lush area of green.

"Oh, that little white speck in the distance? It just left, darling, I'm sorry." He went back to mowing his lawn, laid back and relaxed. Retirement has treated him well.

"Yes, that little white speck in the distance," I sulked.

I walked back to the house.

After Mom heard the news, she was contemptuous towards me, tossing $30 in front of my place setting to pay for a cab. She was indeed dissing me, something she rarely does. Along with Dad, she had about two hours sleep from the grueling trip to Myanmar, evident when she poured espresso in my cereal bowl instead of milk.

'Why are you always so careless about what you do? Do you know how much money your Dad and I have to pay for tuition and

bus fees?" I recall her harsh criticism. I prayed Dad didn't hear the words from the bedroom, where he was sleeping soundly.

This must be what Dominic has to experience daily.

In actuality, it wasn't entirely all my fault, I thought to myself. I was just trying to get rid of a nasty blemish on my nose in the morning by putting some of Mom's cream. I already have enough moles and freckles. The last thing I need is another one of those suckers.

I may be the most insecure girl in the school.

"That was a horrible way to begin the day," I said to myself, trudging to a nearby main thoroughfare to hail a cab.

A rarity. A local hipster driver pulled up to the curb. The man was slightly abnormal and socially awkward, playing loud glam rock music from indie artists. His flamboyant voice irritated me a bit. Typical of Singaporean cab drivers, he loves to chitchat. In local parlance, he would be described as being "kaypoh" (meddlesome, busybody, and overall nosy).

Perhaps I should've hailed an Uber. Cheaper and apparently a policy against chitchatting with riders.

"So, where do you come from?"

I made sure to be smart and not give out too many details: "I was born in Virginia." I'm usually a more interesting person.

"Cool." Then he whipped out his rendition of:

"Country roads, take me home, to the place I belong. West Virginia . . . Doodah, doodah."

"Dude, West Virginia is a separate state from Virginia." I want to say that he mixed up the song with Yankee Doodle as well.

I snapped on my over-the-ear headphones and watched that distorted video over and over again. That was a rather obnoxious yet convenient way to block out the driver's drivel. He might still be talking but I'm disengaged. He knows the destination and I just need to calm down.

Flashbacks of uploading the video last night popped into my mind. Indeed, I felt almighty and guilty at the same time. Uploading the video produced a high dose of adrenaline.

By the time the cab arrived at school, I only had a few minutes to reach homeroom on time. I paid the driver $29 fare and spotted him a $1 tip. He nodded his head in agreement, either to the music or the gratuity, which is usually not required nor expected.

I entered the gates, thinking that the school facilities were going to be bleakly empty. Lo and behold, a clique of five girls catwalked towards me with suspiciously sly-looking faces.

"Bullies," I thought. "Bullies. What do I do in this situation—five against one?"

I knew every single one of these girls. Never once did it occur to me that they would even care to know me. They usually don't even look at me, much less direct words in my vicinity.

"Hey, Sista! Your video has gone viral around the school. Soon enough, you're going to be a real star."

I cursed under my breath.

Jesse Ross, a plump tomboy, brought up the sensitive topic. Although plus-sized, Jesse is still quite popular due to her in-your-face personality. Her crew members are similarly as gregarious.

The others nodded their heads in unison sassily. They literally looked like Bubblegum K-Pop music videos with the standard choreographed automatons with identical smiles and make-up. Just not nearly as pretty.

To them, I'm timid, fragile, and generally untouchable. They're all taller than me, more popular than me, and definitely cheekier than me as well. They steer away from the major sports such as basketball or soccer, dominating the school in other ways, such as cheerleading, volleyball and Student Council.

"No, I won't. That video wasn't meant to be that way. It . . . it was all a brutal mistake by me."

"Brutal mistake? Are you messing with us? This was amazing!"

<u>All of this was said in tandem (Multiple Choice)</u>:

(a) "Far from it, girl, you're the talk of the school."

(b) "Good job in not going anonymous on the posting. Good call."

(c) "I wished I were there instead of you."

(d) "You killed it, genius."

(e) All of the above.

I looked stupid shaking my head and thinking about the video at the same time. Yup. I should have never done this.

Memories Cached

My ruminations continue in the stall.

I was slowly tasting "popular," a path which would not bode well for me in the long run. What if this drags me into the pit of being an infamous kind of popular? I've been tempted to do stupid things before just for the laughs and the attention, and I've done them. Those were insignificant things, though. The rush was amazing.

Two individuals doing their own thing are now implicated in a major scandal. As for popularity, what if it is short-lived? In today's world, viral videos lasting a day are compared with hot videos for a week from the previous year, I thought.

Forget about viral continuing for years. That's reserved for that horse-riding K-Pop guy and those super cute kids on YouTube.

"No," I said, slapping myself in the face repeatedly. Flashes occurred in my brain, triggering too much adrenaline for me to handle. I thought about the fate of Dominic. Then Talinda.

There isn't anything I can do now.

Even if I were to pull the video from YouTube, the video remains forever engrained in the minds of viewers, not to mention on the YouTube servers. For that matter, a few contraband copies might also exist.

I relive these irritating deliberations right here in the stall again. Scary how this amazing memory of mine enables me to track back to that exact surreal moment of entering the popularity crowd.

My heart plummets a mile once I realize that my ultimate fate has been sealed.

"Savannah, stop bawling, you little crybaby," Jesse comes crashing into the bathroom. She and her clique pound on the stall door repeatedly, loosening at least one hinge. "We know you've been hiding from us ever since this morning. You aren't gonna hide anymore."

Instantly I'm forced to stop the crying and the mind games, which yields a rather awkward situation because now I have to pull off a straight face with reddened eyes. I use my uniform sleeve—already tear-drenched to wipe my eyes once more.

I've attracted lots of attention ever since becoming so emotional. I'm a scarecrow, but instead of fending off the birds, I'm attracting them. Never previously well dressed, I am now entirely disheveled.

"Don't be scared—get out of the stall," Jesse interrogates. "Mmm-hmm!" her sidekicks provide a side comment. I turn the knob so Jesse and her clique see "vacant" instead of "occupied."

Odd choice of words in this circumstance. My mind wishes to be vacant but it is fully burdened with disbelief and horror.

The clique cajoles me out of the bathroom, and I see a diverse array of boys crowding around. I am glad they weren't within earshot of the conversation in the bathroom. It's a bad scene, made worse if the other half of the school hears about the hubbub.

Horace makes his way over, with absolute bewilderment on his face. Ryan, the school bully, shoves Horace out of his way rudely. Remarkably, Horace seeks revenge for the shove by punching Ryan as hard as he can, yielding no reaction from Ryan at all.

Ryan barges in front of Jesse, invading my personal space: "What's all the fuss?" He appears perplexed and a bit troubled.

"Nothing," I downplay. Instead of being agitated, I try to be unflustered as more and more people gather. Now is not the time to break down in tears again.

I'm imagining a scenario where I'm a famous celebrity receiving unwanted attention from the media. All the microphones are pointed directly at me. Why me? I just want to go out for a coffee and a bagel unnoticed and like everyone else on the street. Disguises are for nefarious criminals.

"The video you uploaded last night was kind of gross, sort of like this," Horace interjects, sticking out a green-colored tongue. "Compounded by the fact that the resolution was below par." He slurps his watermelon Airhead.

"I haven't seen it. Who were the two smooching in the video?" Ryan questions.

Everyone knows Ryan is intimidating. I remain silent. The crowd remains silent. Radio silence.

Jesse shatters at the face of silence: "Talinda and Dominic, of course!" She pulls me over to her so our hips graze.

"Why would you say that, Jesse?" I say. "And no, I don't want to be in your clique."

"Hold up, hold up. Talinda and who?" Ryan asks.

Before anyone can say anything else, I respond: "No one, no one."

"What?"

"Dom—" Jesse begins. I nudge her so she doesn't continue.

"Wait, who's this insane brat who kissed my sister?" Immediately, Ryan's face turns sour.

This is when realization settles in.

Ryan and Talinda are siblings. Who would've known? There are several kids whose last name is Chang, both Korean and Chinese. I have never seen them speak with one other, ever. But my goodness, they don't look similar!

Everybody remains silent.

Dominic's trouble just multiplied.

"Dominic? I'm going to beat up this kid." Soon enough, Ryan will release waves both of the audible and physical variety. Richter Scale for humans. Luckily, his friends quell him down to the point where I can only hear the seething of his white teeth—the air rushing in and out of the holes in between his slightly gapped front teeth.

"Guys, can we just drop this?" I try to calm the crowd. "The worst possible scenario right now would be either Dominic or Talinda finding out about the video. Besides, class is starting in a

few." I storm off towards my locker, infuriated at the jeopardy I put the couple and myself in.

Everyone stares at me, confused and frowning.

I admit it; that's a lame way to end the conversation. But a dozen intimidating human beings against one? I really had no other choice.

Chapter 5
Summit: Chiang Mai

International schools throughout Asia love to send their kids away for a week in the spring or autumn. Teachers and administrators alike aren't off on holiday as most of them accompany the students on these excursions. Primary schoolers don't travel abroad but hole up in campsites in Singapore or youth hostels by the beach on the East Coast.

The East Coast of Singapore is an interesting welcome for fatigued travelers coming into the city from Changi Airport. Lush greenery predominates along East Coast Parkway, as the seaside is reserved for park space.

Urban legend has it that a portion of the highway can be readied for emergency military aircraft. Removable planters, which separate the divided highway, can be pushed aside to land and deploy fighter aircraft.

For middle schoolers, we're destined to climb the Great Wall and muck around the Summer Palace in Beijing, else it's off to Xi'an to see the terracotta armies. One teacher spooked us last year when he told us over and over that the terracotta armies were actually mummies rather than clay soldiers. Obviously, not a history teacher.

If you look closely at the soldiers in one area, it's hard to find facial expressions exactly the same. After a dozen comparisons, the mind and memory begin to falter and confound.

It's unbelievable that in March 1974 farmer Yang Zhifa accidentally discovered the 2,000-year-old relics when he attempted to dig a well to irrigate the crops of his cooperative farm. Archaeologists eventually found more than 8,000 terracotta warriors.

For years, Yang and a few of his contemporaries sat in the tourist shops near the excavation to sign autographs for tourists, including President Bill Clinton in 1998. Museum officials, recognizing a tremendous publicity and photo opportunity, recruited Yang to meet Clinton, schooling Yang with a few English phrases:

Yang: "Who are you?" [vs. what he was taught, "How are you?"]

Clinton: "I am Hillary's husband."

Yang: "Me too."

Entourage and audience: [laughter].

Local officials: [grimace].

The story has it that Clinton asked for an autograph. Yang, who was illiterate, apparently drew three circles on a piece of paper, to the dismay and embarrassment of the local officials. Following the side trip by Clinton to Xi'an, officials decided to offer Yang a few calligraphy lessons.

When we arrived at the terracotta warriors site and the gift shops, we could not find Mr. Yang nor his autographing colleagues. Pity as selfies would not require literacy in any language.

This year, we're off to Chiang Mai where we will hang out on an elephant refuge and learn how to cook pad thai chicken noodles.

The weeklong excursion is called Summit. You would think it's a chill week but for middle schoolers, it's wake-up calls at daybreak and lights out early. Roll call every hour during the day. Single file but no holding hands required.

It ought to serve as a break for me at least. I just need to get my mind off the Talinda incident.

Worse of all, it's green—well, sort of. Each group leader (teachers of course) confiscates all electronics (smartphones, computers, tablets, phablets, etc.) at the airport before departure. Even iPods (who even owns one these days?) are taboo. Actually, students and parents are asked not to pack these contraband items but most kids try to sneak one or two in their suitcases or backpacks.

In some cases, guys bring two smartphones and give the older one to the leader. Smart.

I didn't pack any prohibited items as I didn't fancy using the device under a blanket in the dead of night.

Cold turkey. No exceptions.

Not really weaned off but force quit.

To recall the events of the Summit trip to Chiang Mai is a daunting task. In daylight, I consciously ignore the debacle. In the wee hours of the night, I forgo REM sleep when I awake suddenly to the memory of Ryan's shenanigans at the Chiang Mai Rainforest Hotel, a three-star property, on the outskirts of Chiang Mai.

A week earlier, during the pre-Summit powwow, Ms. Marlin, who led Team Green, made her intentions clear:

"Dominic, you and David will have to room up with Ryan. We will have the hotel arrange a trundle bed. Offline, Ryan's a bit of a pill to deal with but the Summit teachers and administrators believe you and David can keep a good watch out."

"But, Ms. Marlin—" I uttered.

"Dominic, we trust you and David can work together on this for us." Ms. Marlin stood firm. David fell into a trance, unable to back up my protest.

Crap, I said to myself. Here's the resident bully who launched an assault on Horace the other morning in the amphitheater area of the Middle School. If he's so cavalier about his OTT pranks at school, to what limits would he hold back in the backwoods—err, deep jungles—of Thailand?

Worse yet, to be confined to a small hotel room with only one friend at my side to fend off Ryan.

As if, either of us, or even both of us combined, hold any sway over Ryan.

"What gives?" David asked me quietly once Ms. Marlin moved away.

"I suppose the School thinks we're obedient kids and have some stroke on keeping Ryan in check."

"That's a laugh," David said.

"The joke's on us, bud."

"It was before my time, and also yours, but wasn't that the dude who ate crayolas in the first grade?" David asked.

"Dude, Ryan eating crayons will be least of our worries," I said. "Just the other day, the hooligan tossed an orange peel over the barrier of the fourth floor. Thank goodness, it was just the peel."

"Strike that," David interjected. "It was the entire peel."

"That guy is hardwired differently than a normal kid. He's always looking to incite a small riot. We need to find a new nickname for him. RiotRyan—"

"How about RuckusRyan?" another kid interjected.

"He, of all people, doesn't need a street name to prop up his rep."

Team Green joined Teams Orange and Red in assembling in the amphitheater area prior to loading onto the six buses waiting outside the Middle School entrance. Ryan saunters over to my direction. David hasn't arrived yet as he's perennially late.

"Check this out, boys. I got a care package from my grandma Stateside. She sent over two months' worth of goodies," Ryan beamed. "Just in time, I can finish these in Thailand."

He then flipped his roll-along duffel bag over using the handle, laying the bag on the steps of the amphitheater. Not a shred of clothing in this bag but simply a smorgasbord of sugar-filled paraphernalia, including: Pixy Stix, Kit Kats, an assortment of bubble gum including Bubblicious and Bubble Yum, and most worrying, an entire can of Tropical Punch Kool-Aid.

Enough ingredients to make 34 quarts of the nasty liquid.

"Hey, Ryan, wassup with that Kool-Aid?" Anderson Young quipped. "Didn't your mom tell you that clean water is a scarcity in Chiang Mai, especially at the campsites of the elephant refuge? How are you going to mix up your concoction in the wild?"

"It's cool, that's why the canister includes a scoop. You just dip it in and take it in as you would cough syrup!" Ryan yelled. "Who said you have to add water?"

Ryan demonstrated. He popped off the plastic top and grabbed the ring on the aluminum seal cover. In one movement, he pulled off the metal cover and cast it over to one of his crew for further disposal.

He then heaped a spoonful into his mouth, swallowed and then revealed his tongue, reddened to an out-of-this-world crimson. Or was it a putrid violet?

By this time, David had joined the circle and chimed in: "Hey, Ryan, do you plan to eat any campsite food?"

"Nope, I've got a stash of Jack Links, Slim Jim and Old Trapper beef jerky below the sugar level. Check this out, boys."

The circle of boys all dropped their jaws as if choreographed. David and I exchanged nervous, non-blinking looks.

For a second, I could only think about those two Ziplocs my Mom packed: one enclosed some bran, gluten-free, table wafers and a few boxes of organic raisins; the other, some off-the-shelf meds for my allergies and acne. No sugary snacks in my stash. Not even Xylitol gum—strike that, candy.

David had arrived late, but he had enough time to catch a glimpse at Ryan's rolling junk food pantry. He seemed in awe that Ryan's parents would allow him to do his own packing. Must be a latchkey kid, David thought.

As we boarded the bus, I exhaled a super loud sigh.

Only a few days have passed since I uploaded the kissing episode on YouTube.

Today, we're gathering at school before taking off for Chiang Mai for the Summit trip.

I despise Summit week as I have to face my classmates 24/7. School's a drag but at least you can bask in anonymity for the most part while the teachers rattle on in their lectures. In this environment of cliques, it's easy just to go unnoticed.

Summit is OTT because you have to live among people you do not necessarily associate with. Nor like.

Having three sisters should make it easier but I just prefer predictability and routine. Luckily, Ms. Marlin of Team Green paired me up with Natasha Holton, who's an introvert. I don't think we ever spoken to each other but she's a Facebook friend.

I reckon 30 percent of my FB friends are people I haven't had a conversation with. I would say that's the case for many of my peers. Then again, I only have fewer than 100 friends, a large portion of whom are relatives.

I know some kids have more than a 1,000 friends. I can't imagine keeping up with the Facebook news stream when you have that many friends.

As the Team Green members gather near the amphitheater, I realize that Dominic is heading to Chiang Mai with me. The entire grade goes to Chiang Mai this year. Although some will leave earlier or later and will have different schedules, the activities are identical.

No sign of Talinda in the mix. That's a good thing. I continue to question whether I should have refrained from uploading the kissing incident. Neither Dominic nor Talinda are my rivals nor are they my friends. I had no ulterior motive or any motivation whatsoever.

Teenagers tend to do things without considering ultimate ramifications, or so I'm told. Some kids chase "likes" on FB and YouTube. The latest habit among students is not breaking streaks in Snapchat. Some randomly tag their friends on popular pages just for laughs.

I can't really explain my poor choice in uploading. Or my ongoing choice not to delete the video.

Memories Cached

The Team Green gals gathered in one side of the amphitheater while the boys set up on the other side. In the distance I noticed that Dominic and his crew gathered around Ryan, one of the school's leading bullies. There seems to be some hubbub surrounding Ryan's roll-along suitcase.

Ryan must have some contraband. The teachers and administrators are oblivious. Mr. Sadlowski departed the day before.

I can't imagine Ryan can carry electronics as that is prohibited by school policy. Summit is meant to be a week where the kids are forced to be independent. No phones, computers, not even iPods are allowed.

No news is super news, the administrators and teachers say to the parents. Parents are off limits except for a short call on the last evening before returning to Singapore. Any electronics found will be confiscated. The phones used by teachers and administrators are reserved for emergencies only.

I won't be able to witness the surge in YouTube views and likes.

Chapter 6
Flamethrower

For some inexplicable reason, the flight on SilkAir (a subsidiary of the flagship, Singapore Airlines) up to Chiang Mai was entirely uneventful. Or perhaps I couldn't concentrate as I hadn't slept well the nights previous.

I was in my head, thinking about Talinda too much.

The second recurrent dream was the thought of working with those giant Asian elephants. The closest I've ever come to a real animal was at Kidzworld at the Singapore Zoo but that was confined to farm animals (ponies, goats, rabbits) as the zookeepers could not let us touch the exotics. Even the tropical birds show at Jurong Bird Park gave me the creeps. I am the squeamish type.

The newfound nightmare involved RuckusRyan. The only memory recovered is waking up in beaded sweat.

The buses rolled up to Chiang Mai Rainforest Hotel, which is situated within striking distance of the elephant refuge, one of the top attractions for tourists and student groups alike who flock to Chiang Mai.

As the kids bundled out of the bus, I noticed that Ryan was the only student who did not wait by the bus to retrieve a checked luggage. Instead, he grabbed his carry-on roller duffel bag from the overhead rack and strolled up the steps towards the reception desk.

He must've packed a week's worth of disposables.

Asia Wild Adventures, the Singapore-based organizer of the school trips, had landed earlier and had the room keys readied for the students. Ryan, David and I sprang forward to the elevator banks, only to be summoned back by the proctors. "We're going upstairs to drop off our bags by room numbers," Ms. Marlin commanded with a measly funnel megaphone. It was more of a plastic cone.

Once the elevator doors opened, Ryan made it to the door of Room 302 first, followed by David. Ryan summarily launched himself onto the bed nearest the door and bathroom while David took the other twin bed. I was relegated to the lumpy trundle bed by the balcony window.

"Man, I need to hit the john," David said, moving straight for the toilet.

He didn't realize that the bathroom was partitioned by a window, partially open as the louvers were not closed.

Ryan immediately plastered his face onto the window, made more ludicrous by his uncontrollable lips.

After flushing, David turned around and blushed.

While I used the toilet—this time unimpeded, Ryan immediately inventoried the closet, desk and bureau drawers. The warning on the fire mask (that opening the packaging would incur a cost) did not deter Ryan from donning the apparatus.

"Boys, check this out!" Ryan exclaimed. "I am the Exterminator! Quick, grab the other one, David, and we can be a team."

Time out. There's three of us.

"No way," David said. "That's going to be charged to the room."

As I opened the bathroom door, Ryan lunged out from the closet with the apparatus. My face gushed white.

It was a sign of things to come.

Ryan didn't even try to place the fire mask back into its packaging.

What was worrying was that I noticed two ashtrays in the room, one next to the bedside table and another near a table by the window. Lo and behold, Ryan gave a hideous yelp:

"Waaaaahhhh, we will have a blast tonight. I've got fire gear and flames as well. The dolts on the hotel staff failed to clear out the souvenir matches, my dudes," he declared, pocketing the bounty.

At this point, I didn't know whether to rat him out or keep silent. David and I would abstain without discussion.

Enforcing a curfew and lights out at 10 p.m., Mr. Sanders, the assistant band director, checked our rooms, short of tucking us in.

"Okay, boys? Good to see you are ready for bed. It has been a long day getting here, and tomorrow's jam-packed. We've got an early start so you better hit the sack now."

"Sure thing, Mr. Sanders!" Ryan blurted. He was anxious to get started.

Within half an hour, I was awakened to the sight of a huge multi-colored flame emanating from the bathroom. It wasn't a camping flashlight. Rather, Ryan had lit up his Axe body spray with the matches, courtesy of the Chiang Mai Rainforest Hotel.

Even David, who's a heavy sleeper, awakened to the fiery light.

Ryan had opened the louvers to the internal bathroom window.

"Boys, get up and watch the Flamethrower," Ryan hissed, as he held the deodorant in his left hand as he restarted the flame.

The flame burst with purples, yellows, oranges and reds, fueled by Ryan's pressing the deodorant spray.

Not satisfied and armed with a near-full can of deodorant, Ryan ran out of the bathroom, sprinted over David's bed and then jumped on my trundle bed. He then popped open the balcony window.

The balcony could be his stage.

He looked right, then left, then right again and realized that pretty much the entire student body had fallen asleep by 10:30 or so.

Dissatisfied that David and I would not be an adequate audience, Ryan leaped back into the room and bundled his way through the darkness to spring open the security locks on the hotel door.

He then zigzagged through the corridor away from Mr. Sanders's room, pressing random doorbells until one of the sleepyheads opened up.

Turns out that Horace is also a light sleeper. His roommate was watching some local TV.

"Hey, what are you doing?" he said. "Don't you know it's lights out?"

"Calm down, bud," Ryan admonished.

"If you get caught, strike that—if we get caught, the entire Team Green will get demerits," Horace said. "Don't be that guy, alright? Just don't."

"Screw that," Ryan retorted. "What's wrong with a few more pushups during the obstacle course exercise tomorrow?"

Within seconds, four other doors opened and Ryan summoned the daring ones to enter our room.

"Keep the lights out, boys," Ryan said, looking towards David and myself. "You newbies who've just entered, take a seat on the beds and I will keep you spellbound.

"If Horace is right, I need to ask you to refrain from yelping even if you are astonished by what you're about to see—"

Ryan then entered the bathroom, opened the shower curtain and turned on the shower, full blast.

He then raised his left hand up with a lit match and then pressed the Axe deodorant, causing a three-foot flame to strike against the shower, which extinguished the flame.

Just for additional impact, he lengthened the flame by crouching and shooting the fuel at a steep upward angle.

Oohs and aahs continued. Running out of matches was the only thing stopping Ryan from lighting up the bathroom. The smoke detectors obviously were useless.

Ash residue emptied onto half of the shower floor.

He asked someone to retrieve another box but luckily no one obliged.

They were all shocked, as David and I were.

"Show's over, kids," Ryan said. "Get back to your rooms. And don't try this at home."

No doubt he had done this before. His teacher was YouTube.

At breakfast, the girls gathered in the café. As usual, the gals tend to sit together while the boys gravitate in the other direction. At this age, no boyfriend/girlfriend relationships have been announced, though I heard of some covert activity on the weekends.

The "go-to" place for teens is Universal Studios on Sentosa, though a more low-key place would be to catch a flick at a cinema in a shopping mall. Orchard Road, Singapore's main shopping district, is an obvious choice if you want to be seen.

For school trips, there's a natural separation of the sexes. The exception is when the team leaders ask the students to sit boy/girl/boy/girl during organized lunches, say with local school children.

During bus rides, the boys rule the back of the bus, despite the heat coming off of the back wall of the vehicle and the extra bumpiness from sitting behind the rear wheels set.

High school is entirely different as there are almost as many couples as there are single nerds.

I'm kind of getting along with Natasha, my roommate. She's outgoing and is interested in hearing about my life. She's the popular type.

The next morning, Natasha approached me and said: "Savannah, I overheard in the elevator that the boys on our floor caused a ruckus last night. I'm serious."

"Oh really? I didn't hear a thing. I was sound asleep." I smiled.

"I thought I heard some rumbling in the hallway and some voices. After a few minutes, I heard a few doors open and close. There was some yelling going on and some horseplay."

"The boys are playing with fire as demerits or worse may be imposed," I remarked.

"Savannah, surely, you are joking."

"What? What do you mean?"

"Well, I heard that someone was playing with matches," Natasha said. "You're a mind reader."

Chapter 7
Downward Spiral

The next morning, David and I made it a point to rush to the hotel café at the break of dawn.

The shenanigans from the previous evening took its toll on Ryan. He snored away as we changed, washed up and brushed our teeth. For a second, I thought it might be worthwhile to turn off Ryan's alarm to cause his tardiness.

But then again, we're talking about the resident bully.

David and I grabbed plates at the buffet, mostly Western fare but some Thai delicacies. Those of us who live in Asia are spoiled with extravagant buffets. It's not just a trolley with sneeze guards but four or five tables with various course selections, such as breakfast cereals, breads/pastries, hot dishes both western and Asian, juices, etc.

It's Thanksgiving on a daily basis.

No omelet chef on this occasion as it's a three-star hotel.

"Whoa, what's up with that stack?" David asked. He wasn't referring to my pancakes but my bacon slices, piled three high, three across.

"Nine, I think. I don't get the good stuff at home so I need to get my bi-yearly allowance now," I responded. "In any event, didn't you get the memo? We are going into the jungle today and won't be back until tomorrow night."

"True. I'm headed back to the waffle/pancake table. Yep, it might be a reprieve from Ryan. Do you know if we have to share a tent with him?"

"You kidding?" I said. "We have to share a tent with Ryan and seven other kids."

By the time Ryan sauntered down to breakfast, it was time to head back to the room to pack an overnight bag. For the next 36 hours or so, we would be holed up in an elephant refuge in the mountains near Chiang Mai.

Instead of a modern hotel, we would be roughing it with bucket showers and sleeping in tents. The bucket showers were basically showers with a bucket perched atop each stall. The user is provisioned with one bucket of water, which is a luxury in rural Thailand.

No Wi-Fi, no interconnectivity whatsoever.

As if we had our smartphones with us.

To compensate for the otherwise spoiled nature of students at my school, the wiser adults decided decades ago that service should be integral to the curriculum. As part of the Summit trip, we are tasked to serve the underprivileged, the defenseless and the abandoned.

At the elephant refuge, we will be learning to comfort the majestic animals, including feeding and bathing them. Though some commercial elephant farms allow visitors to ride the elephants, our sanctuary will not allow that as interestingly, elephants' spines are not built to support humans riding on their backs.

However, the refuge leaders may take us on limited excursions through a short track near the refuge. Some of us would be able to lead the elephants on foot.

After a two-hour drive through windy roads north of Chiang Mai, we arrived at the sanctuary, a joint operation between Chiang Mai locals and the Karen hill-tribes. The latter are the people whom you might have seen in a NatGeo or BBC special. The Karen women have elongated necks, sporting brass rings on their necks, shins and forearms.

Almost all of the students gawked when we arrived at a nearby Karen village. The teachers had all led trips here so they were accustomed to the sight.

I was glad for once that no one could take photos or selfies. For that matter, the only kid with a camera (Horace was an exception as he was the school's resident photographer) was reluctant to take more than a few photos. Even those were shot from a distance.

Horace was out of his element. As most of us were.

The Asia Wild Adventures guide mentioned that he saw a Karen woman with more than two dozen rings on his previous trip. Even a dozen seemed daunting.

We could not fathom the daily suffrage encountered by the Karen women due to this cultural tradition. It rings of the women in ancient China with bound feet.

After an hour in the Karen village, we moved next door to the entrance of the elephant refuge.

"Welcome," Khun Veera (meaning "brave") stated. He was the lead trainer and caretaker of the animals. Not a Karen tribe member but a Chiang Mai local, Khun Veera doubled as a veterinarian.

"In the next few hours and through most of the day tomorrow, you will have a unique opportunity to live with the elephants. My team and I will teach you how to work with the elephants and take care of them.

"Many of these beautiful animals have been abandoned or are endangered by poaching."

In the corner of my eye, I could see Ryan looking forward to the experience. He would not be fazed.

"The first thing you need to know is about safety," Khun Veera stated. "Because you are young, you will have limited exposure to the adult males at our farm. But you will be able to feed and bathe a couple of our younger elephants."

After a few hours working with the smaller elephants near the thatched roof structure, Team Green was exhausted. Mr. Sanders led Team Green to the canteen at the outdoor encampment.

We were so famished that we didn't really taste the food served on banana leaves. No utensils were offered so we had to eat with our hands.

"That was good," Ryan said as we made our way to the tents. "I call dibs on the first cot!"

David and I made sure that we took the cots farthest away from Ryan. I made a special note that the 10-man tent had a semi-open flap in the back for a quick exit.

"What the hell?" Horace screamed. It wasn't even daybreak and the roosters were still fast asleep.

Horace jumped up and started swatting his face, then his arms, midriff and legs. At one point, he ran out of the tent and ran to the nearby shower. Only on his fifth attempt did he find a half bucket of water to drench his body.

Red ants. Utter commotion.

Someone had poured Sprite on Horace's pillow overnight and some other sticky stuff from the tent opening to his cot.

Mr. Sanders, who surveyed the situation, was not pleased. He warned Team Green boys that kitchen cleanup duty would be on tap if no one admitted guilt.

That's the international school way. One infraction by an individual means an entire group is in the doghouse. That said, no one had any evidence who was the culprit. Or so they said.

I suspect that the guilty one had ingenuously used condiments from the evening meal. No streaky Kool-Aid or melted Kit Kats.

As usual, I said nothing, did nothing. The same goes for the rest of the crew in that tent.

Peer pressure.

Nope, Ryan pressure.

For the morning activity, Team Green was depleted by one-fourth. Half of the boys were called to duty cleaning dishes and cutting vegetables for the luncheon. Ms. Marlin mentioned there were some troublemakers last night.

Come to think of it, I recalled seeing a tortured Horace, drenched and with red marks on his face and body, running through the campsite.

The teachers and administrators were absolutely oblivious to the flamethrower episode. Perhaps they didn't want to admit that neither they nor the hotel management had prudently removed the matchbooks from the hotel rooms.

The invasion of the red ants upon Horace's cot must've been a ridiculously funny sight. But then again, this is real life and bugs in jungle can be poisonous.

Neither Ms. Marlin nor Mr. Sanders were able to extract a confession from the Team Green Boys tent. As a result, they were assigned to kitchen detail as a punishment.

They missed a great segment as we joined Khun Veera for his periodic vaccinations of some weaker elephants. He also showed us how to feed vitamins to the baby elephants, disguising the large pills in fruits and large vegetables.

Someone had the audacity to ask whether elephants like the King of Fruits, the durian.

"Funny. Actually, some elephants eat fallen durian," Khun Veera suggested.

No way, most of the students responded. Some of us didn't know that durians have a prickly outer shell that would compete favorably against pineapples.

"How about the Queen of Fruits, the rambutan?" Jesse asked.

"Haha. Sure, the rambutan has a softer shell," Khun Veera responded.

Chapter 8
Encore Performance(s)

After a full day at a local school that catered to underprivileged children, Team Green retired to the Chiang Mai Rainforest Hotel for the last night before returning home to Singapore.

Every other day or so, Mr. Sanders would allow Team Green to break away from the hotel for a 30-minute jaunt to pick up toiletries or a quick bite. We were instructed to go with at least two others if we ventured off the hotel premises.

While others ran off to KFC or the local pharmacy, Ryan headed directly to Tesco Lotus Express, a convenience store that competes with 7-Eleven. He needed to replenish his sugar supply.

I joined a few kids for a snack at KFC and found my way back to the hotel room. David was in the shower and Ryan was loitering near David's bed.

Out of the blue, he hopped on David's bed, dropped his shorts and urinated on David's pillow. Just for good measure, he then splashed the hotel phone on the bedside table.

I couldn't believe what I just saw.

"Hey, don't do that," I pleaded.

"Shut up, or I'll punch you."

"That ain't cool, Ryan. What did David do to you to deserve that?"

"Nothing. But that's not the point."

I did an about-face and left the room. For the better part of half an hour, I paced the hallway, frantically at first. I tired quickly and then just sat down against the window at the end of the hallway.

No fewer than two dozen classmates passed by, wondering why I was in shock, sitting on the window ledge. If I were at school, I could bury my head into a book or stare at my mobile phone. Staying at a three-star hotel, I couldn't find a newspaper to stare at.

Should I rat out Ryan or let it slide? How could I not protect David? It's one thing to invite ants to Horace's pillow but to pee on David's pillow? That's entirely another crisis.

Sure, our school has known banter and its share of pranks. It's a sign of close friendship. But this?

Mr. Sanders whisked by. He seemed to be in a hurry to return to this room and call it a night.

"Hey, Dom, how ya doing?" he said. "Time to hit the hay. Have a good one."

I offered him an upside down smile. Opportunity missed.

Horace, sporting a bathrobe and hotel slippers, passed by. He had visited the infirmary to receive some ointment for his bug bites. Poor chap.

No opportunity there, though I would have traded places with him.

My buddy, Archie, who was in Team Red, wandered by. He had the same schedule as Team Green but arrived a day later and the order of activities varied.

"My man! Glad to see you. What's up?" he exclaimed. I remembered I was mad at him for getting me into trouble the other day. But I pretended to act as if nothing was wrong.

"I never thought I would see you. I'm staying on the floor above but I'm down here because I need to return some playing cards to this kid. We just got back from the elephant sanctuary."

I kind of wanted to confide in him about the Ryan episode. Or was that episode(s)?

"Hey, I need to talk to you about something."

"Sure, bud, what's up?"

For three seconds, I balked. He probably thought I was going to bring up Talinda.

"Never mind, I'll catch up with you in Singapore."

"Sure, when are you leaving?"

"Tomorrow, first thing."

"See ya. Cheerio."

I returned to the room. Pajama'd up, David was watching TV from desk chair while Ryan was rearranging his stash of candy and snacks as if nothing happened.

That night, students could receive calls from their parents. It would be our only contact with our parents during the entire week.

I hurried to the bathroom and jumped in the shower. The phone rang; David picked up.

I grimaced.

"Dom, it's for you."

Thank goodness there's a phone near the toilet. I spoke ever so softly into the receiver.

"Hey, Honey," Mom said. "Dad is beside me so we'll just keep it short. How are you doing? How has your week been?"

"It's been alright," I mustered. "I am a bit tired."

"Naturally so," Mom said. "Well, get some good rest and we'll see you at the airport arrivals tomorrow."

"Mom?"

"Yes, son?"

"Never mind, see you tomorrow."

"Okay, bye."

"Bye."

Click.

I returned to the main room while David went to the bathroom to brush his teeth. Ryan stepped out of the room to chat with one of buddies.

Now was my chance. I hadn't thought about it but it just occurred to me.

I grabbed David's pillow and tossed it below my trundle bed. I then whisked my pillow onto David's bed.

There wasn't an extra pillow in the closet so I had to fashion a headrest with my bed sheet. I pray that I wouldn't be found out.

To ensure this, I switched off the main lights by the doorway, avoiding the switch on the nightstand between the two twin beds.

"Boys, what's up with the lights out? Let's party on our last night."

"Ryan, I'm crashing. It's been a horrid week," I said.

"Yeah, man, let's call it," David said. "Mr. Sanders will swing by soon."

"Wussies! After roll call, I'm going over to my crew's room to play poker. We need a fourth. Who's in?"

"I'm out," I said.

"Same here," David responded. He was fast asleep in three minutes.

Neither David nor I could not muster the courage to rat out Ryan as we were intimidated by him. Never could we have imagined we would confront such a situation at our age.

Between the first night in the hotel and the seventh day of the trip, David and I tallied up the egregious antics of Ryan, some of which were witnessed and some of which were hearsay:

- pouring Sprite at the base of Horace's pillow so that he would get a wake-up call from a platoon of red ants,
- sneaking into an adjoining room and ordering room service for four diners while the crew played cards in our room,
- placing rocks in Savannah's backpack before the 5-km hike,
- emptying a bottle of shampoo in one of the shower buckets, and
- playing Flamethrower with deodorant spray.

The shampoo gag was also based upon a YouTube favorite. Of course, there was an additional egregious act: peeing on David's pillow and the hotel phone.

I felt hopeless, both in my lack of courage to confront Ryan and my inability to warn David. At least I switched out his pillow.

To this day, I never told David what happened. To this day, I can't remember how many times Ryan had the hotel room to himself. No doubt he inflicted further visible and invisible damage to hotel property.

The next morning, I almost teared up as I packed my bag for the trip home. For some reason, David was especially animated. He had a most restful sleep. I didn't have the heart to tell him what happened.

It pangs me to this day that I did not report Ryan's antics at the time it happened. No doubt the proctors would have sent him a red card for lighting the deodorant on fire. A teacher would have had to accompany him home straight away.

David and I were good acquaintances but not close. Even if I had the gumption to rat out Ryan, I wasn't sure I wanted to be known as a snitch. If only David and I had the guts to speak up after the Flamethrower episode. Double snitches.

Memories Cached

Okay, it was David's fault as much as it was mine.

Upon return to Singapore Changi Airport, I met up with my parents at the arrivals hall in the cavernous Terminal 2. We hugged it out and then walked toward the parking lot.

"How was the trip, Dominic?" Mom asked.

"It was alright, a bit tiring," I said.

"How so? Too many hikes in the deep jungles of Thailand? You didn't like the camping?" Dad asked.

"All of that and then some," I responded.

I claimed fatigue and feigned napping as I sat in the backseat. Mom and Dad discussed something else and I drifted in a constant mad remembrance. I couldn't stop thinking about the incidents that occurred, some of which were downright dangerous and all of which were rude.

That night, after lights out, I knocked on Dad's study and beckoned for a chitchat.

If I didn't inform my parents about the Talinda predicament, at the very least, I had to tell Dad about this.

After all I had been through, I still didn't.

I was on the receiving end of a prank by the boys on the last day before departure.

Shortly after breakfast, we bundled onto two buses to a countryside school that served the underprivileged. The children were absolutely gratified to meet us. Although a few of them could say a few words of greeting and gratitude, most of the kids blessed us with their vibrant smiles. Many children sported eyes that gleamed throughout the day.

After lunch, the school administrators and teachers led us and the schoolchildren on a short hike up a mountain path.

The children, many of whom walked miles to school, made the trek without carrying water. We spoiled international students carried backpacks with toiletries, snacks and water.

For some reason, after a half hour of hiking, I languished and fell behind the pack.

"Savannah, are you alright?" Ms. Marlin asked.

"A bit winded," I responded. "I don't know why. It must be the tropical heat and humidity."

"Your backpack seems a bit lumpy," Ms. Marlin noted.

I paused to take off my backpack. She was right. The bottom of the pack seemed off-kilter.

I opened the outer compartment to find a banana leaf wrapped around three rocks.

I had been duped.

The first person who came to mind was Ryan.

Who else?

Pretty good prank but the laugh's on me. I played dumb once I reached the destination with the rest of Team Green.

Famished and sweaty, I made my way to where the boys congregated.

"Savannah, you're the last to arrive. You've been eliminated from this stage of the race!" Ryan pronounced. No one laughed as no one knew of Ryan's latest antics.

"It wasn't a race, you idiot."

I let it go.

Dominic overheard the exchange, glanced at my reaction and then turned away. He was all knowing. Little did he know that Ryan would be on the warpath soon.

Chapter 9

Some Looks Exchanged

Back to the real school grind.

Good news—Chinese class is almost over. Once the bell rings for recess, I can finally relax and rejuvenate in the library. Right now, Wu Lao Shi (Chinese for Teacher Wu), my Putonghua instructor, is giving the class a pop quiz of the characters we had learned over the past week in preparation of our upcoming unit test.

"Crackkkkkkk" goes my back as I grab the back of my chair with both hands while turning 160 degrees to my left.

"Mr. Chiu, enough of that!"

Yet again, Wu Lao Shi scolds me for cracking my back too loudly.

Oddly, my parents cannot crack their knuckles, much less crack a back. I guess I inherited the flex gene from an earlier generation. They say cracking joints too often is detrimental to my overall well-being, as it may cause the earlier onset of arthritis in later years.

Online websites contradict this, saying that cracking one's back is just "nitrogen rushing to the spinal cord," or something along those lines.

Is that scolding really necessary? Or is Wu Lao Shi purposely trying to ruin my social reputation in front of my classmates? Obviously, ever-pedantic Wu doesn't care. Nor do my useless classmates. They just sit there in their chairs, with blank expressions on their faces.

No doubt they are having more fun in French or Spanish class, bringing food, having parties and all. Although a billion and a half speak Chinese, and another half a billion want to learn the most popular language, the romance languages seem more interesting.

Buddy Chao, a know-it-all, self-centered kid, resists the temptation to unleash his customary ghastly laugh. He's a carbon copy of Riley Smith. The girls in the class alter their expressions between glares and frowns, with occasional bug-eyed and cross-eyed looks.

"Students, please turn to page 37."

Oh no, not this chapter again. The students have to recite words from a tale regarding a cow complaining about his problems to a farmer.

I can't believe I'm wasting my time reading foolish fantasy stories.

This makes far more sense in Chinese than in English because the Chinese love to depict anthropomorphic animals in stories.

Not a fan.

George Orwell's satirical "Animal Farm" is an exception to this rule, except that he was commentating on the lead up to Communism rather than simply teaching a foreign language.

For God-knows-what-reason, I was enrolled in a German international school in primary school. Maybe that could explain why I missed out on Chinese at an earlier age.

German was taught through the use of a bear as the main character. Now this bear had a good ol' time. He not only lived in the woods but also went supermarket shopping, not to mention a trip to the amusement park. Now how is that germane?

But Wu Lao Shi's cow story is horrendous.

"Eenie Meenie Minie Mo (complemented, of course, by the Chinese version)," Wu Lao Shi murmurs, pretending that he's picking a person at random. He must have a toddler at home.

The hypocritical Wu speaks at least these four words of kiddie English. He says we can't utter a word of English in his class. If any student spouts such a word, severe extra homework consequences for the entire class will follow.

How cold is that? One innocent mistake by the called on student and the entire class is reprimanded. Problem is, you can't remain silent and shrug nor even say: "Wo bu zhi dao (I haven't the faintest idea)."

Little do I know, Wu has me in his sights.

Wu's eyes are laser guns, shooting red beams of light: "Dominic, you're up. Stand. What was wrong with the cow in the story?"

Why me? Out of all the people in the class, why did you choose me?

Shoot. I didn't study at all for this impromptu pop quiz. Wu Lao Shi is very unpredictable.

For the record, why am I in the second-most advanced Chinese class in our grade? Without Mom's drill-sergeant parenting, I would be close to the bottom of the class.

This tells me she wasn't training me hard enough this week.

I wish I could have Mom by my side right now, just whispering every Chinese character in my ear.

I seek refuge from Wu Lao Shi's tirades through Mom's guidance.

Unfortunately, all I can muster is: "I don't know." Admitting I had not studied for this pop quiz seems like the most suitable option. I choose the honest option.

"Dominic, sit down. Next question: why was the farmer so negligent in his actions? What did he do to irritate the cow?" Wu Lao Shi bellows in his usual tone, placing his mug down. "Hmm?"

I sigh, knowing that studying last night would have made all the difference. I'm blessed with the ability to memorize characters for the sole purpose of the next day's test. Though Chinese, I am handicapped as our entire family speaks English at home. Even my parents speak English to one another.

Putonghua is not my mother tongue. Due to the lack of repetition and immersion in a Chinese-language environment, I data dump that week's information once I complete a test. Come finals, I have less than a 20 percent retention rate.

Buddy Chao contemplates over this question. He returns to his Auguste Rodin's "The Thinker" posture. In a few seconds, he's going to form a Tiger Woods goatee due to the recurrent stroking of his chin.

His chin-hairs are stimulated. Can Buddy cough up the answer?

"Umm," Buddy chimes. Query whether "umm" constitutes Putonghua.

His raised stiff arm shoots up at an angle. Spastic, one might describe. Gunner Mainland China transplant.

Buddy nods up and down as he arches his back. The entire class prays that Wu Lao Shi calls on him.

Wu Lao Shi barely notices. He has a tendency to ignore those who hog the front seats. His beige turtleneck camouflages the similar-colored desk. Boasting a staggering height of 6-foot 4, he would have to look down and pull off a quadruple-chin if he were to notice Buddy, sitting a few meters in front of him.

"I guess it's time for some Popsicle sticks," he murmurs after only five seconds. Each student's name is written on a Popsicle stick, all of which are placed in a wooden cup. It's sort of like the fortuneteller's sticks at the Buddhist temple but no good luck can be predicted.

Buddy wants to inflict an outburst but is still hopeful for the mere 1/15 chance he might get selected.

Whoops. The gal not wearing school uniform, Shelly Duanmu, gets picked. Shelly's last name is a rarity; almost all Chinese surnames are single syllabic. She's preoccupied, chewing the pink goo off her fingernails, ripping everything off.

Apparently, Shelly told her homeroom teacher that her school uniforms were in the wash. Sounds like my tired excuse for being late to school. Shelly's cool though, as her grades will forever remain below mine.

Man, this is going to be more entertaining than my Star Sports TV at home.

"Shelly, could you respond to my question in Chinese?" Wu asks politely, though his tone yields sarcasm.

Alarmed, Shelly uses her Wolverine fingernails to flip the pages of her Chinese textbook. She strategically bit the sides of her fingernails so the middle section is pointed and exposed. I make a self-note not to get within three meters of her.

Shelly's still flipping the pages. I would be flipping out by now if I were her. Shelly couldn't care less.

"Wo . . . ting bu dong (I don't understand)."

Rough day.

"Zao gao (Oh no)," Wu Lao Shi shakes his head, which finally causes Shelly to perk up. The whole class laughs.

"An jing (quiet down)!" Wu Lao Shi admonishes.

Come to think of it, how do you say "chill out" in Chinese? It could come in handy on my next school trip to China.

Wu Lao Shi hiccups, then draws another Popsicle stick out.

I'm unclear of the answer. However, ironically, I'm hoping he chooses me because I just want to get out of here.

"Mr. Chiu," he enunciates.

The whole class glares at me. Buddy exasperates. This is my curtain call.

Drum roll, everyone.

"[In broken Putonghua] Frankly, I don't know what the cow's complaining about. In real life, animals can't speak like humans, unless you're interpreting the Bible." Woah. Did I actually just say that?

Buddy pummels the desk with his fist and laughs, making all sorts of clamorous noises. "That's so accurate."

Wu Lao Shi appears startled at my overwhelming outburst. He is at a loss for words.

Yes, Wu Lao Shi, I am correct. You have a brand new teacher's pet. Just kidding.

Wu Lao Shi gives me the death stare, holds it perfectly for three solid seconds, and then the bell rings.

The meaning behind the three-second death stare is hard to perceive. Is that a signal that I could be in trouble for the showboating? Nah. I toss that idea into my mind's trash bin.

"Guys, we will focus on these words some more next time," Wu Lao Shi examines his watch, only noticing now that the class is two minutes late for break.

"All students are dismissed."

Yes. Finally. I snatch all my school supplies out of my desk's cubbyhole and bolt towards the door.

"Except Dominic."

You're kidding.

I approach Wu Lao Shi with an irked expression; he thinks I'm in denial for what I did wrong.

He gravitates towards the whiteboard and scowls at me (little does he know that his perfectly ironed beige turtleneck has an ink spot below the pocket, thanks to a leaky pen). Should I let him know? Is time of the essence when it comes to extracting ink from a cotton shirt?

"Was that really necessary?" he asks. My mind starts to wander off as he begins spitting out quick-fire Chinese. Am I supposed to respond or is he blabbering to himself? Someone used to tell me that the quickest way to learning a foreign language is to learn the quick-fire words first.

Another dude told me to learn the curse words first. Much more memorable.

Shock value, my friends.

Not a good time to suggest this to Wu Lao Shi.

I'm nodding in front of him, pretending I understand every single word he says. Every few seconds, he veers off topic into an unfamiliar Chinese dialect. I begin to glance at my surroundings. There's a couple of signs next to the doorway explaining common Chinese words, such as the seasons. For example, here's dong tian (Winter): 冬天.

The writing structure is relatively simple; a kind of two-armed octopus on top, followed by two leaves on the bottom. At least that's how I see it in my mind. Obviously, my logic defies all standard rules of Chinese calligraphy.

I've also heard that most Chinese characters are symbols that signify the meaning of the word. Where in the world did that come from? I don't quite understand. How is a two-armed octopus followed by two parallel leaves supposed to signify "winter?"

Sometimes, I don't understand the dudes who invented these set principles. Not to mention, there are longhand Chinese characters, otherwise known as traditional characters, and the reformed Chinese characters, otherwise known as simplified characters.

Whoever came up with the idea of Pinyin and the four tones? The first tone resembles a high note in music. The second tone is slightly lower. The third is the lowest possible tone. Finally, the fourth is an accented one.

And oh, great, the Cantonese dialect, which predominates in Hong Kong and Guangdong, China, boasts nine not-so-distinct tones.

Mom thinks I can't correctly articulate the first tone correctly. Excuse me for not being in choir. I specialize in the clarinet.

As Wu Lao Shi finally lets off most of his steam, I use my peripheral vision to check the bottom of the glass door to see who's outside—I can tell who people are just by checking their shoes.

Shoot! Archie's showing off some red Air Jordan sandals, and I know it's him. He's also exhibiting his signature narcissistic pacing.

Wu concludes his lengthy harangue by pointing his finger towards the door. I've retained absolutely nada from that episode. I am free to go.

Looks as if the parent-conferences won't be all that great. Tell me something new.

Dominic approaches me in the most awkward way possible—at least I think he does. He dashes out of his Chinese class for some odd reason, perhaps to fetch a friend. After opening his classroom door, he slams into me, knocking me over.

Geez, is the kid a rugby player? His shoulder is massive!

"Sorry," he mutters. That was an insincere remark. He doesn't even offer to give me a hand to assist. Instead, he looks at me for two more seconds, slightly dazed, then proceeds to chase Archie.

My face is flat on the ground in an attempt to keep my identity obscure. The dirty concrete makes contact with my skin. Of course, my face hates me.

"Is there blood on my face?" my left cheek asks my right cheek.

"No, a pimple popped," my right cheek giggles. It's probably not true but it sure does feel like it.

This feels horrible.

I get back up on my feet, making sure that Dominic has left. I can ill afford for that kid to get a good look at my face.

Chapter 10
Squirm

Bad news. Coach Cory Jenkins, today's substitute for the Social Studies teacher Mrs. Parker, is about to send the class contingent of nerds to Mr. Sadlowski's office as they were caught fantasizing over their League of Legends characters on Skype video chat while he was lecturing about the three branches of U.S. government.

These nerds can be pretty comical. They do stupid things, unaware of the possible ramifications. Mom tells me that the smartest people in the world usually have the least common sense.

Now that I think of it, I agree. Geniuses live a life of opposite extremes.

Come to think of it, I think I have pretty poor common sense as well. Mom likes to call it: "EQ." I shouldn't have roasted poor Wu Lao Shi, nor should I have kissed Talinda.

That makes me a quasi-genius. Haha.

What's even more comical is the idea of Coach Jenkins rambling on about U.S. government. Instead, he should stick to marketing and promoting his YouTube channel, which features him pulling off Frisbee trick shots. He's nothing compared to my guy, Brodie Smith.

By the way, Coach Jenkins double times as my P.E. teacher. Mr. Sadlowski randomly selected him to take Mrs. Parker's place as she called in sick today.

Little did Coach Jenkins know that Mrs. Parker failed to prepare a lesson plan. He's incompetent at ad-lib presentations.

"Hello? Samuel? Hi! It's Cory. I have three students I need to send up. Yes. I caught them video chatting on Skype, discussing League of Legends characters. Yes. They will head up to your office shortly."

Pause. Coach Jenkins hangs up and tosses his phone onto a stack of papers on Mrs. Parker's desk.

Super awkward silence.

"Get out of here, now! Go straight to the sixth floor. I've had enough of you three!" he urges the incorrigibles.

This is the epitome of Coach Jenkins, as we know it. He's as stern as my Dad, and yelling is about all he's good at.

If the students in this class were smart, they would attentively listen to Jenkins' warnings and pray for a quick, relatively painless, escape.

Nope. Not happening in our class. These three students video chatted each other despite being in the same classroom.

Ed Cho is another classic example. To catch a few Z's, he makes perfect use of his binder by placing it in front of his face in between him and Coach Jenkins. Cho has a way of shutting his eyes when the lecturer is facing the whiteboard, somehow opening his eyes when he or she turns around. He does this over and over until he gets caught.

My library copy of "The Catcher In The Rye" is open and placed on the ground between my feet. My head is arched forward and resting on my desk. I'm not too big on reading but I need to finish this novel for my final book club meeting tomorrow. Dad encourages me to read a range of novels in my spare time, but I'm mostly preoccupied with other hobbies. I'm only motivated when I read the classics. I'm even more motivated when I have a specific deadline to complete a book.

I am relegated to completing homework in class.

"So . . . where were we? Oh. We're talking about checks and balances, right?" Mr. Jenkins returns. "Ed, can you please listen? You're even less attentive in Social Studies than you are in my P.E. class."

Ed's personal record on the mile run is 8:52 minutes. I think he complained the other day that his P.E. grade was bringing his GPA down. Now, P.E., out of all subjects bringing that GPA down? Ouch.

"Sorry, Mr. Jenkins," Ed says as he tips his binder over. It descends and hits the floor.

"Okay, let's try this again. The three branches (Executive, Legislative and Judicial) check and balance one another to ensure no branch overpowers another. For example, if the U.S. President, as the top leader in the executive branch, exercises his power to veto a bill, he is checking the powers of the legislative branch.

"Do you kids play bridge, the card game? It's sort of like the trump suit called by the declarer."

Not a single student perks up when Coach Jenkins offers this analogy.

"Ahem," he continues. "However, the legislative branch can override that veto with two-thirds vote of both houses (that is, the House of Representatives and the Senate). Another example of a check and a balance would be the judicial branch over the legislative branch, whereby the Supreme Court can overturn a law legislated by Congress that is deemed to be unconstitutional. The Supreme Court can also hold unconstitutional certain Executive Orders issued by the President."

Okay, it's easy to see Coach Jenkins is reading off a website he Googled earlier, interjecting some offhand and misplaced commentary here and there. Now, he turns to the impeachment process, whereby the House has the sole power to impeach while the Senate is the sole court for impeachment trials.

"Hey, does anyone know whether President Bill Clinton was impeached?" Coach Jenkins inquires, again to blank faces.

Sitting behind Archie, I nudge him and whisper: "Dude, I got something to ask you outside."

"What?" Archie asks. Luckily, his voice does not break. We sit in the peanut gallery.

"Later."

"You guys seem apathetic. If you're going to come in class with this lazy and unfocused attitude, I'm not going to help you," Coach Jenkins complains.

In P.E. class, Coach talks about the importance of having a good attitude all the time.

"For the record, and if any of you care to take down a note or two, the former Arkansas Governor was saved from impeachment as the Senate did not reach a two-third majority required for his downfall."

Silence.

"Okay," Archie says, nodding his head because he feels bad. Bless his heart, but that was awkward.

"You know what? Class is dismissed."

Dismissed? It's 2:53—12 minutes early. I'll take it.

Archie is the first one to exit the classroom. The peanut gallery is nearest the door.

Wow. I'm quite surprised. Getting dismissed that early is a one-off experience that even most of the high schoolers cannot get in their school careers. The only thing that comes close is a troublemaker like Ryan yanking the fire alarm. Sure, it's happened before.

Archie and I head to the nearby supermarket. I grab some ginger ale, a chocolate bar and a bag of chips for the bus ride.

"Have you asked out your crush yet?"

"What?" Archie looks surprised. "Since when did this come about?"

I hate it when my friends act in denial.

"We were discussing this next to the planter the other day. If I kissed Talinda, then you would ask out your crush, right? Wait, who even is your crush?"

"I don't have a crush. This was all banter. See, I lured you in. You made a huge mistake kissing Talinda."

"Why?"

"Think about it. What's her last name?"

"Chang."

"And what is, uh, Ryan's last name?"

"Chang . . . wait. Are you trying to tell me that they are siblings?"

"You're not wrong about that."

"But how could you be so sure? There are about 20 people in our grade with that surname."

"Trust me, I know. I scanned their Facebook profiles and I noticed that they are biologically related."

"Oh, gosh, shut up. How does he know that I kissed Talinda?"

"That doesn't matter. You should hide from Ryan. Don't let him bully you. Whenever possible, I'll cover for you. Look, it's going to be uncomfortable because both of you were roommates, but you're going to be fine."

"Dang. Yeah, we were roommates."

Head down, I say "dang" five extra times.

Suddenly, I look up and see some wild thing. I notice a girl hiding her face with her black jersey. At a first glance she looks like one of those nefarious criminals I see on TV.

She is intentionally trying to keep at a distance from me. Her personal boundary is pretty extreme.

"Who is that?" I question Archie.

"I don't know. She seems like the spectator that joined me when you kissed Talinda."

Wait a minute. She seems familiar. I don't quite know her actual face to be sure though. Forget about knowing her name. I remember the same girl looking totally and unnecessarily distraught outside the Chinese classroom today. Then again, a few of the girls are like that in our school.

These are young, insecure, weird girls.

"Hello? Anybody there?" I say as both of us approach her at the fruits section. She ignores and slithers away.

She is one abnormal girl.

Archie and I purchase our snacks and head to the bus roundabout. "I'll Skype chat you tonight," I say. We have some more things to discuss. Late."

Okay, time to get on the bus, Chiu.

As most kids on this bus know, neither the bus driver nor Madame Tang, the bus mother, allow any sort of food or drink on the bus. Hmm. How do you eat potato chips quietly?

Whoops, yet another one of my pathetic mistakes.

Madame Tang hops from her seat as I enter the bus. I bet she's dabbling on Flappy Bird, trying ever so hard to beat her high score of 15.

Yep, I was right. Flappy Bird plummets to his death as bus mother nearly drops her phone on the floor upon discovering the infraction.

Looks as if I made myself pretty clear that I was going to start my own party on the bus.

"Jalapeño chips and a monstrous chocolate bar? And over there a ginger ale?" Madame Tang might get a heart attack.

Riley, the only other kid on the bus pulls his antennas out and further assesses the situation.

"None of these shall be allowed on the bus! Do clearly you understand me?" Madame bellows. She's creative in her placement of the adverbs. She pauses, signaling that she either:

1) wants to throw **my food** away, or

2) wants to share **my food** with the bus driver.

Of course, none of the above should be allowed.

Well, perhaps I don't have a choice. Bus mother shoots me a chili-red glare, as if she's craving for my jalapeño chips fried in peanut oil. How sad it really is for me to squander my snacks and to donate them to the self-anointed "arbiter of human decency." Let's just call her that.

Silent but dead set on taking the snacks, Madame Tang grabs a ratty box reserved for this purpose.

"Yeah, you just go ahead and take all my food. Take everything. Be my guest," I say, squeezing these eats into bus mother's hands.

Both bus driver and bus mother are flabbergasted. They've never seen so many snacks confiscated in one taking.

"The unopened items will be donated to the less fortunate," Madame Tang says, unexpectedly. "Thank you."

"Sure," I respond. Then, I head over to Riley's seat.

"You know, you could have just stuffed those snacks in your backpack as you entered the bus," Riley chimes in. "She wouldn't have noticed. But now that she caught you in the act, she's going to be suspicious every time you board the bus."

"Not so fast, Riley. She told me that my donations would surely go to charity," I say sarcastically.

"Do you really believe her? She's probably going to stuff herself with your snacks once she gets home."

That was the joke.

I sit in my seat, far away from Riley's seat.

Please don't come closer, Riley.

He comes closer.

Dominic, one thing. What makes you bond with Talinda?" Riley asks me out of nowhere.

"What?" I pretend I didn't hear that.

"You know, bond. Covalently bonded." Great. He had just learned something in science class, and he related this to my predicament.

It just so happens that as Riley uttered this question, a horde of high schoolers boarded the bus.

"Why would you suddenly bring this topic up?" I say, turning my voice down several notches.

He snickers and snorts a bit, before finally saying: "Dude? Have you been hiding under a rock lately? You have been quite the hot topic at school. Don't you know?"

I suddenly perk up. I'm no longer famished.

"Dude, I won't be surprised most of the school knows that you kissed Talinda."

I'm panicking right now. My spine tingles.

"Kissed? Riley, back to earth, please. We're only 14. We can't fall in love that soon." I hate lying.

"You two must be very mature 14-year-olds. Haven't you seen the video loaded by Bodacious18?"

Suppose not.

"Bodacious18?" I asked. "Who's that?" It appears that Summit has delayed my access to YouTube and the general gossip at large.

"It's that Savannah gal. Savannah Dixon. It's funny because the YouTube name is ironic. She named herself 'Bodacious18' so that no one would think it's her. It didn't work."

Whoa, Savannah Dixon? I stop to think for a second. Who? Why would she do such a thing? To take the video is bad enough. But to upload it onto YouTube is another! Stomped! Stomp is the local equivalent of YouTube in Singapore, but the difference is that Stomp mainly focuses on irrational human behavior.

The rational side of my mind then takes over. I've altered my perspective. I can feel a quiet anger building inside of me.

The main infraction was my PDA episode. But cyberbullying is an entirely different matter.

The episode is online! How could this happen?

Once I arrived, I thanked Riley for informing me, then rushed out of the bus as fast as possible.

I can't believe I'm constantly messing everything up right now. How could I possibly be stupid enough to walk within the area of a few meters of the person whom I most want to avoid? Gosh, apart from my first ever basketball tournament, I've never been more insecure.

Yeah, it was sixth grade. The ragtag girls' basketball team got a reprieve from school on a Friday to participate in a basketball tournament held at the Australian International School. No fewer than a dozen international schools joined.

For some reason, Coach Mila Swanson gave me the nod to start as the weak side forward. I suppose she noted that I attended every practice and was a team player.

At tip-off, our star player, Melissa Chan, tapped the ball hard in my direction. I jumped to retrieve it but missed, so I ran back to retrieve it.

I blamed it on skipping the rancid lunch served in the cafeteria or the glare off the side window in the unfamiliar gymnasium.

After snagging the ball, I glanced at Coach Swanson, who appeared to be waving her arms wildly, like a fledgling bird attempting flight.

I summarily ran toward the wrong basket and scored a nice lay-up for the other team. Own goal, they say, in soccer—ahem, football.

Sheer and utter disbelief and embarrassment all around when it comes to basketball.

I was benched at the earliest opportunity where I remained for the remainder of the game. Final score: 28-27 in favor of the Australian gals. Not nice. Double ouch.

Indirectly responsible for the team's first round loss and knock-out from the round robin tournament.

So much for my short-lived career as a student basketball player. We even had to go back to school after the lunch hour.

This time, I remember the look on Dominic's face when I tried to hide my identity twice. I should have brought a surgical mask to school or disguised myself as someone. But I don't really look like anyone. At least I don't look like anyone special. If I tried to look like someone else, I would just make a big, fat fool of myself. I would become a pseudo-girl.

I kinda wished my folks would move out of the island-state. Moving houses would not help as I could always be bussed to school. Pray my Dad gets a job transfer somewhere. Hong Kong is fine; Beijing, too polluted. Myanmar is problematic but entirely doable in the current state of affairs.

Chapter 11

A Real Distress Call

Thank goodness Riley brought up this issue before it got out of hand. This is atrocious. How could someone simply get away with posting a video of my incident with Talinda? Now, I'm becoming a notorious figure in Singapore International School.

My guess is that most of the students in my grade know about this—Riley noted that the video amassed more than 1,000 views in just two days. Who exactly is Savannah Dixon, that girl hiding behind the screen with the eerie username "Bodacious18"?

I make a formal checklist of the incidents, first-hand:

- ✓ Talinda and Dominic, the latter prodded by Archie, break rule 102 of the Student Handbook, which clearly prohibits all students from partaking in PDAs.
- ✓ Mr. Sadlowski pronounces that we are path-makers in our breach of rule 102—the first-ever in the 40-year history of the school.
- ✓ Some fiend called "Bodacious18" videoed the event surreptitiously, indirectly breaching rule 143, which states, in effect, that no student should ridicule or belittle another student through her direct or indirect actions. This rule is part of the anti-bullying section.
- ✓ I later find out Bodacious18 is actually Savannah Dixon.

- ✓ Mr. Sadlowski has found me out but I haven't divulged Talinda's name. Talinda's is not clearly visible in the ruddy video capture. I don't know if she has been interrogated. And certainly, I did not conspire with "Bodacious18" and am clearly the target of cyber bullying via social media.
- ✓ Mom doesn't know.
- ✓ Dad doesn't know.
- ✓ Mom will find out first and then tell Dad. Uh-oh.

I anticipate three words: "How was school?" This is the phrase that usually welcomes me back home, along with a bear hug and a spring roll. If it's a special day, Mom might add in "Honeybunchee" as well. That's how mundane my afternoons usually are.

What does she expect me to say? School sucks, but life is not much better. Pudgy has the best life.

I yank open the front door of the house. Pudgy approaches me and barks in an innocent, muffled tone. Dog language is always easy to understand. They are able to act and communicate in a similar way that humans do.

Shockingly, I don't hear any greeting whatsoever from Mom.

Pudgy directs me to the master bedroom. On the way, I notice my sister Erin's bedroom door is ajar. Her face and her long neck stretch out the door.

"You're in deep trouble. Watch out."

I then approach the master bedroom where Mom sits upright on her seat, looking at me in total disgust. Set at full brightness, her computer shows a paused video.

"Are you kidding me right now? Look at this." Mom spins around and looks directly into my eyes.

This leaves me speechless. Mom's probably certain that I've seen this suspicious video, even though I haven't.

"Do you have any idea about the trouble you're getting into? Heck, do you even have the slightest idea?"

"Mom," I begin, but she interrupts.

"Have you even seen this video? In case you haven't, you need to sit down and observe every detail here."

I glance over to the side of the screen. Gosh. This video has more than 3,000 views. Mediocre by YouTube standards, but outrageously viral for just the school.

Time out. The enrollment of the entire school totals only 1,250 students; middle school enrollment is capped at only 600 students. It's been shared and re-watched multiple times.

"Answer me when I say something. Don't give me that attitude. Look into my eyes and tell me what's going on."

The scolding reaches a new threshold of repetition. Ad nauseam. Add nausea. Suddenly I'm airsick, seasick and carsick, though I'm standing on solid ground. I want to puke.

"Mom, I actually have never seen this video at all. I swear." This is one of the few instances that I sincerely speak the truth. I'm serious. The school has a no smartphone policy. No phones in class. Most of us check our phones before and after school. And during lunchtime.

And for the previous week, I've been holed up as a captive in a hotel room with Talinda's brother in Thailand.

Of course, Mom does not buy it: "Do you expect me to believe that, Son?" I hate it when she identifies me other than my given name. No chance it will be "Honeybunchee" today.

The 34-second video commences shortly afterwards, proving to be more soul destroying than Mom's lengthy harangue. At 19 seconds into the video, I'm cringing at the sight of the kiss with Talinda. Although the video is highly pixelated, "Bodacious18" does a magnificent job of zooming in on the subjects. Only the back of Talinda's head is visible.

For goodness sake, the kiss was a light peck. It was the result of immature teenage shenanigans, no more, no less. Why does everyone have to blow it out of proportion?

Mom presses the space bar on her keyboard pretty darn hard. If she breaks it, it will come out of my allowance.

"First of all, what in the world did I tell you in the first place? Right now, I want you to say the five mottos **loud** and **clear**."

Oh yes. The five mottos Mom has been taunting me—ahem, teaching me—with ever since elementary school. Even my cousins have been introduced the list and can recite it on demand. Here I go (caps utilized for emphasis):

1) NO PAIN, NO GAIN
2) YOU SNOOZE, YOU LOSE [Note the "IF" is purposely deleted]
3) BE DISCIPLINED
4) NO GIRLS
5) NO DRUGS

The last one's a given; Singapore has a no-excuses, first-strike death penalty for drug possession.

I imagine Mom's going to add a few more to the list of mottos here. Clearly there's not enough, in my opinion. Perhaps Mom chooses to leave it like this for the near future, as she wants to keep everything simple and straight to the point. Point number four is the most important, according to Mom, to which I highly disagree.

"Say the fourth point one more time, loud and clear!"

"No girls," I say feebly.

"Not good enough."

Ugh. "NO GIRLS!" I scream to the top of my lungs. I now picture Erin falling onto the carpet laughing away. She usually is on the tail end of a scolding. And I don't understand why she gets a boyfriend, no questions asked.

"And Be Disciplined!" Mom booms. "That means if you got to do it, do it at the right time."

My bad, I forgot to relate Rule 3 with Rule 4.

Mom and I have had this discussion many times previous. She says girlfriends can wait until not only after graduation but after I make a few million. If med school is in my future (not likely now), that means four years of college, four years of med school, a few years of residency depending upon selection of specialization; specialist training for good measure. That's 29ish, give or take a year or two or three. Then again you can go somewhere in the Midwest and do a 6-year combined college and med school program.

Other boys are preparing for their coming out via cotillion. I've never applied to Mom for such a radical extra-curricular. She would reject on the spot, without consulting anyone. Remember, no girls.

"That's right. Now tell me, who is that girl you are smooching? Tell me everything. Spill the beans," Mom loves that phrase. "If you don't say everything right now, Dad will have to intervene."

That makes me gulp. A gulp the size of a snake's mouth with a mouse inside.

"First of all, the girl's name is Talinda—"

Mom interrupts straight away, which just irks me so much. "What's her last name?"

"Uh, Chang."

"Chang, huh? Is that Chinese or Korean? Local Singaporean, Taiwanese or Hong Kong? Mainland gal? ABC (American Born Chinese) or KBK (Korean Born Korean)?" She fires away, exhausting most Asian countries and permutations. "Alright, go on."

I'm not getting engaged, much less married here.

"She's really nice and kind, but a bit insecure. I liked her a lot at the time, but I don't quite know about now." Oops, why did I have to say that about my current lack of feelings for Talinda? Mom won't like that.

My sentence fluency starts to collapse as I murmur words incoherently. Finally, my words fade to a complete stop. I pretend nothing happens.

Mom looks particularly bored and unconvinced: "Go on?"

Is that a command, or a request?

I can hear Erin's continuous snickering behind in the background. That distinct laugh is an Erin Chiu special.

"Erin, this stuff is meant to be private, not to be discussed right in front of you," I say. I wish Mom would ask Erin to shut her door, as if it would make any difference.

"Go on," Mom commands. She could care less if Erin hears. Or the neighbors for that matter. They might already know the subject matter.

"You heard her. Go on," Erin butts in from afar.

Why are you two ganging up on me? I think to myself. I really detest the feeling of facing the inquisition.

"She's intelligent, trustworthy and overall just a great person."

"Enough on that. I want to know more about the kiss. How did all of this happen?"

Erin is now well situated to hear the entire scoop.

"I planned the whole thing out. I did."

This was a lie.

Archie actually dared me to kiss, and I succumbed to that dare. Gosh. How dare he did that?

Like my false confession to Mr. Sadlowski during that meeting, this lie is working to my disadvantage. Before, I would actually blame friends for incidents related to me.

Mom wouldn't buy that. If she did, then she would tell me to stop being friends with the person.

I lied this time because I just didn't want Mom to extinguish my friendship with Archie. As turbulent the family may be at times, at least I might be able to count on my friends.

I also neglect to mention that in some ways, Talinda is equally culpable as she teased me with the ongoing "TBH" saga and its related points system. Truth be told, if I had said Archie and/or Talinda had peer-pressured me into this, Mom would go further ballistic.

So yup, I lied twice.

If I commit a misdemeanor, Mom and Dad will eventually forgive me because I'm their only son. The chance of my parents forgiving one of my friends' misdemeanors is very slim.

One of the characters in my Chinese name means "honest." And to lie only proves the law of irony.

Weirdly enough, I think by lying, Mom actually believed me. What I said, though false, is what she wanted to hear.

"Oh, so this time, you are telling the truth," Mom raises her eyebrows in approval. I can now see Erin peering through the master bedroom door, as she mimics

Mom's expressions and hand movements. I'm practically seeing double.

"Now, what's the school's reaction to all of this?" Mom now asks the toughest question.

"Umm, well, Mr. Sadlowski caught me leaving the amphitheater after the kiss."

"Isn't he the P.E. teacher?"

"Nope, he is the Assistant Principal."

"Oh, yeah, the one with the wife who wears loud clothes. Got it."

Pudgy is in the living room, barking continuously.

"What's Pudgy doing?" Mom says, and then exits the room.

Thank goodness I do not need to go into the details of my dreaded discussion with Mr. Sadlowski. That would have been a further disaster.

"Ha!" Erin approaches me, and then elbows me in the gut. "You kissed Talinda Chang? No way! This is not happening right now!"

She collapses on the ground, with a distinctively loud thump. She's having a field day and can't wait to catch up on the latest scuttlebutt with her boyfriend. He'll probably ask for the modern day autograph—a selfie with Dominic for Instagram. I can picture it: Erin's boyfriend standing next to me with his two fingers primed for a photobomb behind my head.

My eyes roll back and forth. I want to bounce something sarcastic back at Erin, but my mind can't think of the perfect retort.

Erin keeps giggling and giggling. Suddenly, I hear a loud "BANG!" of the front door. Uh oh. That's probably Dad. I can tell by his clamorous footsteps, even when barefoot. Pudgy spins out of control.

Erin mouths: "That ain't good. He's home at 5:00."

Yes, it's Dad.

First, he stomps into the master bedroom without saying a word. That's the most agonizing part. He takes off his tie and hangs it in one of the closets. He flops himself on the bed and exhales a massive sigh.

"You know for sure I usually don't come home at 5 p.m., right?"

"Yes, Dad." Dad insists I call him "Dad" formally every time I acknowledge him, even when not during a lecture.

I glance over to Mom, who appears cross to me and attentive to Dad. Then, I glance over to Erin, who finally seems like she's feeling sorry for me. Perhaps not.

"Dominic, I assume you know exactly what I'm about to say."

"Yes, Dad, I know," I remain somber.

"That's it?" Dad yells. "That's all you got? I expect you to be crying right now."

Erin probably wants to cry with me, just because she's been yelled at in the past by my parents and she can relate to my situation now. But Erin won't start crying until I start crying.

The horrible thing is, the situation I am in right now is much worse than all of Erin's situations, multiplied. Frankly, Erin has probably done more egregious things, especially on school property, but she never gets caught.

What's more agonizing about this situation is that Dad hasn't said a single word regarding kissing, smooching, being under aged or anything of that nature. It's more agonizing than being yelled at my face.

C'mon, cry. Keep crying. Unfortunately, I'm not at all good at crying. My eyes drip insincere tears. Mom shakes her head.

This session drags on for two long hours.

Unremarkable is my return home. I manage to board the bus on time, taking a seat toward the front with the students from elementary school. Sometimes I like to stare at them and wonder about their absolute innocence.

By when does a young person turn on her peers?

For what reason does a girl resent other girls and guys?

Is it caused by a single event or a series of circumstances?

Can the urge to harass, cajole or ridicule be overcome?

Is the urge more dangerous when possessed by a single person or a group?

Is the urge originating within the body or the mind?

Through my early years, I was never part of a clique or tried to join one. Occasionally, a handful of girls would try to befriend me. However, for the most part, I never followed up beyond that first approach.

It's not that I don't like people, but certain people are real pests.

I'm trying my best to let go of the thought but I can't. I have this weird feeling that Dominic has seen the video by now.

Again, I can't explain why I videoed Dominic and Talinda the other day. Was it out of curiosity? Certainly it was not revenge as I didn't know either well at all. Neither one had been obnoxious to me.

Then again, Dominic was quite brusque when he mowed me down outside of the Chinese classroom. But that was well after that epic video.

Chapter 12
An Unwanted and Unnecessary Apology

Soon enough, Dad escorts me to the nearby desk, and wakes up the computer. I sit on this monstrous brown leather "throne."

"Look away," Dad mutters as he begins to type the administrator password. Erin and I are forbidden to know Mom and Dad's password. We are only allowed to use this computer under only the most extenuating of circumstances.

I believe it's necessary to mention that my parents not only know our passwords, but also have fingerprint access to our iPhones.

"Parental Controls" on the desktop is similar to that of an Arizona Maximum Security Prison. On this computer, Erin can't Tweet, Facebook or Instagram. At the same time, I can't play FIFA, PGA Golf or Call-Of-Duty Modern Warfare 2. So basically, this is like equal rights between the two of us.

"Turn back here," Dad says. "You're not an owl, for goodness sake." Was that a reference to my flexible neck?

"Answer me," he insists.

"Ahem. Yes, Dad."

Dad pulls up the browser, and then goes to my e-mail. He knows my username and password from heart.

"Here," he says, as he hands me the keyboard and mouse. My Inbox shows one new e-mail addressed to me, copied to my parents, strongly depicted in bold black letters:

3:03 PM, March 3, 2015
From: SAMUEL SADLOWSKI
Re: KISSING INCIDENT

"Look at that. Those bold black letters sure do scream, don't they?"

"Yes, Dad."

"That's rhetorical. Now go ahead and read it. As a matter of a fact, read it out loud so the whole house can hear you."

Why? Just why do I have to do this? I clear my throat.

Just before that, I have one more follow-up question to ask Dad: "Does Mom know about the e-mail?"

"Of course she knows. You know her. There's nothing privileged in this house."

Stupid question.

I commence reading the e-mail. Here goes:

Dear Mr. and Mrs. Chiu:

I am writing this to you this afternoon to inform you of an unfortunate and unacceptable incident that occurred on February 16.

As I walked towards the amphitheater, I found Dominic suspiciously behind one of the pillars. I accompanied Dominic up to my office straight after for questioning. After some interrogation, Dominic finally conjured up the nerve to speak the truth: that he kissed a girl from his grade, behind that pillar. I was taken aback, that Dominic and his partner would have the audacity to engage in a potential breach of the Student Code.

During our meeting, I questioned him about the incident. If his partner had not run away, the discussion would have been a lot easier. Now, I have to further question Dominic in a later appointment about the identity of this girl, something that I feel obligated to be doing as an Assistant Principal.

In this meeting, I reiterated Article 102 of the Student Handbook, which reads:

> It is important that students demonstrate an attitude and behavior regarding interpersonal relationships that would be acceptable to people of various cultural, ethnic and religious backgrounds. Students must refrain from inappropriate behavior

> such as intimate and prolonged embraces, kissing and similar actions that may be offensive to the general public.

For your reference, no student, in the history of Singapore International School, has committed a breach of this rule, ever. After this incident, however, I must say that this school's good name and reputation has been damaged.

An anonymous person uploaded a video to YouTube, which became viral in our school, within a few days. It has now spread to other schools and throughout the island-state. Despite the poor 240p quality, the video amassed more than 3,000 views.

I am extremely disappointed in Dominic's behavior, especially as I know what a responsible and intelligent student he is. Last year, he was Treasurer of his grade, taking part in numerous leadership roles. This incident is highly unacceptable. Dominic needs to lead by example and make the right choices and decisions, which may affect him in the future.

I hope you will speak to Dominic about his use of time in school. Dominic should know that the amphitheater, or any other unsupervised facilities, is strictly prohibited for any activities after school. As both of us approach the middle of the second semester, I hope we can work together to get him back on the right track.

Please feel free to contact me if you have any concerns or questions.

Regards,

Samuel Sadlowski
Assistant Principal
Singapore International School

I stop to take a deep breath. I know Dad is capable of exploding at any time.

He snatches the mouse and moves the cursor over to the "reply" button. "Here's what I want you to do. I'm going to need to you reply back to Mr. Sadlowski and apologize for your mistakes. Your mother and I will arrange an appointment with him sometime later."

"When will that be?" I ask.

"Mom, go check the planner. I believe parent-teacher conferences are just around the corner, right Dominic?" Dad taps me on the shoulder blade. "Haven't they told you multiple times in homeroom?"

"Yeah, well sort of," I mumble. I can't be bothered to raise my voice because Dad will shut me down even more.

"What do you mean by that? It's either a yes or a no answer," Dad insists.

"Yes." I actually knew that parent-teacher conferences were coming up.

Mom barges in with her desktop planner. It is three times the size of the regular student planner.

"Dominic, it looks like the parent conferences are actually next Wednesday through Friday, March 11-13. Erin, the same goes for you."

"Oh, phew, so we get to skip three days of school? Yes!" Erin exclaims from the other room. As a B/C sophomore in high school, she is willing to make use of every opportunity to take a day off.

"Not really, Erin. Mind you, Wednesday is still a half-day of school. We're hoping to meet with your high school teachers after we speak to Dominic's teachers and Mr. Sadlowski," Dad insists, exuding a big sigh. "Do your thing, Dominic. Reply to Mr. Sadlowski."

I can't. I just can't.

Nobody has the idea of how utterly hostile I feel towards Mr. Sadlowski. Every single word that comes out from that e-mail ricochets inside my heart with guttural power. Mr. Sadlowski is blowing things out of proportion—no different than any other adult out there.

"How in the world do I reply to this?" I mean to say to myself, but instead Dad overhears it.

He gives me a nonchalant shrug. "Make sure you make it as apologetic as possible."

"Roger that," I mumble, not showing a single sign of enthusiasm. I reread the e-mail once again, and then once again for good measure.

"So . . ." I say, fingers perched well onto the keyboard. As one of my symptoms of laziness, my fingers splay across the keys as I press a bunch of random letters, like this series: **alekfjerderf.**

Hey, can't they make QWERTY produce entire sentences on demand?

Good thing my parents exited the room, as I now can really focus. I muddle through:

Dear Mr. Sadlowski:

I sincerely apologize for my inappropriate behavior at the amphitheater after school. I should never have kissed a girl behind the amphitheater pillar. Not only was this a breach of Article 102 of the Student Handbook regarding Public Displays of Affection, this was also an action completely incompatible with my age and maturity.

. . . [press here for more]

Not.

I have no idea what to say after that. I video call Erin on Skype, who is online. She is only a few meters away, nestled in her bedroom.

This is basically what the gamers did when Coach Jenkins substituted for the Social Studies teacher.

Within seconds, she picks up. Ah, vintage Erin, forever glued to her social media.

"Yo, you could have just walked over to my room to talk to me. But nooooo. You instead choose to video call me."

"That doesn't even matter. Look, I'm trying to get this e-mail over with. Could you please help me?"

"Me? Kinda funny you say that because I'm not a good writer."

"We all know that," I giggle sarcastically.

When you roast yourself and your brother agrees to the roast. Classic.

No mercy is shown for her computer's trackpad as she exerts tremendous force with her index finger, thus exiting the call.

"No! Come on, Erin!" I yell.

"Later, Mater," she replies.

I can hear Dad's rhythmic marching steps entering this room. He scans the screen to see how many paragraphs I wrote while he was gone.

"One paragraph. One paragraph? I've been helping Mom in the kitchen for several minutes now. C'mon. Hurry up."

"Oh—" I say. A teenager's standard response when scolded.

"Actually, take a break," Dad shoos me away. "Go do your homework or something productive. Then come back later."

"Thanks, Dad," I whisper awkwardly, almost inaudibly.

Nah, Dad wouldn't have heard that. I need to say that a bit more clearly. "Thanks, Dad."

"Yeah, you said that twice already."

I'm lying on my bed, with nothing much to do except think about parent-teacher conferences (PTCs), which are coming up soon.

As I attempt to move on from the stress of the video upload, a few other hypotheticals pop up in my mind: What if he hunts me down to confront me on my ill-fated decision? And what if we're miraculously placed in the same classes next year?

Mom has registered for all of my PTCs to be on the last day, Friday—in fact in the afternoon. I was able to maneuver Mom into this schedule so that I would not have to bump into Dominic during the PTCs. Hopefully, my strategy pans out.

I'm not fond of any class I'm currently taking, other than Film and Media Arts, or maybe Social Studies. The first is an elective (I couldn't get into Chef I) and the other's a required course.

Film and Media is always an easy thing for me: video some footage, edit and then finally present the movie. I enjoy both shooting the video with my father's DSLR and using the editing software from iMovie.

Social Studies class just requires kids to memorize key events in history. Nothing much. The only issue is that the Social Studies syllabus jumps around a lot. One month we're discussing the Civil Rights Movement of the 1960s, followed by Native Americans. Weren't the natives there first?

As far as I know, I stand on the middle rung of the ladder based upon academic achievement for the majority of my classes. I'm neither outstanding nor a target of any teacher's initiatives. In other words, I like to hover below the radar. So at the PTCs, there probably won't be much to talk about.

Kind of like my usual social life. I'm neither here nor there. Sure, the cool kids who hang out every Friday night don't like the nerds and gamers. But I'm normally unknown in the school. At least the gamers have each other.

PTCs are organized like speed dating. Teachers sit at desks no farther than three meters apart. Parents, in tandem with their kids, make the rounds around the gymnasium. It's 10 minutes per session so it's ideal if your parents book meetings back-to-back during the peak hours so that none of your teachers have a gap in between their appointments.

Mom and Dad have never spoke to me once about my grades or overall progress during this semester. They aren't really the inspiring type. Rather than staying at home, they are often traveling to places I have never been to, like Italy, Iceland, or Indochina. And Myanmar.

I think many people could sympathize with me on trivial matters, such as being the third sister of four. The eldest sister and the youngest have it good but Sister2 and Sister3 are lopped together as middle sisters. I don't quite stand out in front of my parents.

These seemingly trivial matters mean to the most to me; they are matters that I dwell upon all the time.

I am totally different than my sisters. The eldest is intelligent and studious. Sister2 is pretty and bound to make the cheerleading squad. Baby Sis is athletic and smart—the best of both worlds. They call them student-athletes. As such, I don't really talk to any of my sisters.

I wish I had the ability to talk to my sisters. Confiding in them would be a much safer thing to do rather than talking to Mom or

Dad, as they could begin to question me, or make fun of me, or even scold me.

I would love to have a baby brother. A miniature person who would cheer me up when I am sad.

Not to stereotype, but I notice many Asian kids in our school don't have any siblings. I wonder what it would be like to live that way. There could be more personal freedom. Actually, maybe not. There would be more parental attention, which may or may not be a good thing. As with most families with an only child, the parents are much too overprotective.

Not good regarding my situation. If I were an only child, my parents would boycott trips to the charity places and stay at home, tutoring and feeding me.

At the dinner table, Dad often talked about how the Chinese have this rule of a "one-child policy," in which every household in China can only have one child. This was implemented to control the ever-growing population in that populous country. I understand that China has now altered that policy in order to ensure a younger population who can take care of its ever-increasing older generations.

Yup, I can't imagine being an only child.

Yet, I often feel alone.

Chapter 13

Omen

Friday, March 13, 2015. Third and final day of Parent-Teacher Conferences.

Oh, look, Friday the 13th. This is a bad, bad omen. And I'm not trying to start a diary over here, but I purposely bolded the above words to set the tone for the day: dark, austere and frightening.

Chinese folks, especially the older ones and especially the Cantonese, highly prize geomancy and feng shui. In fact, property developers in Hong Kong are notorious for excluding certain floors in buildings, such as the fourth (which in Chinese sounds like "death") and the 13th, which is equally inauspicious.

Oddly, one could live on the 50th floor of a high rise, which in fact would be only 30-something stories tall. Developers have a tendency to exclude the 40th through 49th floors for the reasons stated above.

Listen, I'm not really a big fan of this kind of lame "Friday the 13th" superstition, but when most other kids and adults keep pondering on this matter, it's kind of hard not to slide in with the crowd.

So today, I should watch my back to make sure no one is messing with me.

For now, my reputation is messing with me. My parents are still furious about the incident but their emotions are in check when in front of large crowds.

I am standing at the entrance to the gym, where conferences are being set up. Besides me, three other families admire the gorgeous view outside. A preppy British kid (probably a sixth grader) dons a checkered shirt with a bowtie. But, I must say, his pants game is on point if you're into preppy-dom. During PTCs, students are allowed to free dress.

Next to that family is Shelly Duanmu, the girl who is abysmal at Chinese. There she is, again, biting her fingernails.

I have to admit. I was guilty of doing that back in the third grade. Once, I ripped the whole nail plate by just chewing it off. The worst part? I swallowed it.

Ms. Gardner, my teacher at the time, gave me a gold star during the last month of school when she noticed I wasn't biting my nails anymore. I was actually pretty proud of myself.

There's also Tammy Moodley, that irksome teenybopper on my bus who always has something to complain about. Yeah, there's nothing much to say about her.

A large A3-sized seating chart of each and every teacher's position is nicely hung up on the signboard.

Dad is parking the car. Erin follows me from behind, easily distracted by her Instagram followers and rising likes.

"Come on, Erin! You're so slow," I complain.

Erin raises her head for the first time in the past half-hour. She must have a bit of neck pain. "Huh?" She resumes her fixation, toying with Snapchat filters.

Here comes the dreaded selfie.

"Are you really taking a selfie?" I shake my head. "I swear, do not ever waste your money and time trying out a selfie stick. I honestly cringe when seeing one."

"I'm still going to get one."

"Where's Mom, by the way?" I ask, just as we enter the near-empty gym.

"Oh yeah, she's one of the volunteers for the Booster Club. She and a bunch of other mothers are catering for all of the parents and students."

"Is she actually?" Oh my goodness. What is going on right now?

This is definitely not a good thing. I can't even begin to tell about all the potential disasters just waiting to happen. For one thing, all my classmates (even friends) who know about the incident could tell their parents, who could then ask Mom about it. That's when I can officially kiss my previously solid image goodbye.

"Are you okay?" Erin asks, but not in a worried state.

"Yeah, I'm fine. Just a little stressed. You know how it is, parent-teacher conferences."

"You can't talk, Dominic. High school is ten times more stressful," she asserts.

Erin is emotionless, kind of like she doesn't care. Most girls her age would be slightly compassionate to a kid stressed out like this.

Why does Erin have to be so indifferent and aloof?

Just then, Dad arrives. "Just finished parking the car. It was hard enough to find a space, Geez. Now, I believe we are one of the first slots for the PTCs."

Mom and a bunch of other mothers casually stand around at their booth, beginning conversations with one another.

"Mom, what are you doing here?" I ask, agitated.

"Excuse me?"

"Listen Mom, I need you to remember one thing. Just one thing."

"What's that?"

I hint to Mom by nodding my head for her to step away from the booth so that we could have a private caucus. She finally obliges.

"Listen, please don't tell anyone about that incident."

"What incident?"

"You know . . ."

Oh, that. Yeah, I know."

"Okay, good."

"Anyways," Mom continues. "About that. Don't you worry." Honeybunchee is no longer in her vocabulary. Surprisingly, she reaches over the table to pat my back. "Here, have some of my cookies. But don't take too many. Save some for the other students."

Oh, yes. I can spot Mom's wholesome oatmeal, macadamia nut and raisin cookies not only because they look good, but also because they smell amazing and will probably taste even better. I am hungry and I have that urge to just munch them down.

"Those look fantastic," I say.

Mom turns her back towards me, giving me that rare chance to grab a handful of those. Like most other people, I have a knack for overeating, especially when I feel scared. I stick about two and a half oatmeal cookies in my napkin. I wanted four but I feel uneasy carrying around a big cache of food. I'd better finish these before any teacher sees them.

"Yo, let's go find a seat, shall we? We are meeting your Chinese teacher first." Dad seems pretty bored, checking his BlackBerry and texting every now and then. Probably the only guy on the street with a physical keyboard in Singapore.

Right about now, hordes of people start piling into the gymnasium. I can already feel tensions rising as more and more kids begin to snicker at me. I won't be surprised that the video-taking girl is here as well, just hiding every bit of her face so I won't bark at her. But so far, no one really looks suspicious at all.

As Dad, Erin and I take a seat near Wu Lao Shi's desk, I notice he's conferencing with Shelly and her parents. He's strict enough to berate her in front of her parents. She seems like a stone cold ice sculpture, thoroughly unfazed by the episode.

I try not to eavesdrop on their conversation, but it's not easy.

"Okay, let's take a look at Shelly's past exam," Wu Lao Shi lifts Shelly's paper in the air, marked with clashes of red markings. She left a lot of spaces blank. "I think this says it all."

The front page didn't show the grade. What if her results were so appalling that Wu Lao Shi put "IE" (Insufficient Evidence)? Optically, that sounds far better than a D or an F.

Suddenly, Shelly begins to bite her fingernails.

"Mrs. Duanmu, Shelly is clearly not trying her very best in class," Wu Lao Shi asserts.

"Hey, who's that girl over there?" Dad questions. He equates nail-biting with thumb-sucking.

"No one special," I laugh. Not because it's funny, only because it's just downright sad.

"No, actually, who is that?"

"That's just this girl in my Chinese class who's struggling," I reply.

I get up from my chair and head over to the Booster Club booths to get more delicious eats. My goodness, I am starving. I trust there's no quota to be imposed on me.

Just then, I notice Ryan Chang enter the gymnasium.

For the past few days, I have tried to pay as little attention to that infamous kid, Ryan Chang. But now, all the bad memories of Summit flood back.

"Oh, man," I whisper under my own breath, squinting my eyes, crossing my fingers and hoping that he doesn't notice me. I still keep strolling casually towards the booth.

But for me, the more casual I walk, the more awkward it looks. At least from my point of view.

Shoot. Archie promised he was going to cover for me. Where is that kid when I need him the most? I need someone to run interference right now. I always thought British kids are adept at combat fighting. Archie is agile, adventurous and has a knack for dangerous things.

I arrive at the table to grab a drink of water, just to find out that Mom isn't there. I feel a surge of anxiety.

Suddenly, Ryan passes by, and almost knocks me over. At first, I almost pretend as if I did not notice the incursion.

This is my first mistake.

My second and worst mistake is greeting Ryan with the words: "Hey, what's up?" and reaching out for a half-hearted fist bump. He then karate-chops my right wrist, which puts me in a weird state of imbalance. For some reason, the force causes me to fall to my knees.

"Get up," he says while prodding me in the ribs.

Ryan isn't quite the buff and muscular type. He doesn't take protein supplements, mind you. He's just a short-tempered, almost stout kid who thinks he's massive. Every time he takes off his shirt, everybody thinks he has a six-pack because his body shape—or perhaps it is his skin tone—really exaggerates his abs. Girls are bound to make comments on abs:

- "Dude, are those abs real?"
- "I don't see any love handles."
- "Why can't my boyfriend get rid of his love handles?"
- "You could grate cheese on those abs!"

But really, Ryan's 5-foot 5, and I'm a good 5-foot 7.

The adrenaline is pumping right away, but I'm not exactly looking for a fight. I've seen those improvised fistfights in Kung Fu Panda and maybe even a few Bruce Lee movies, so I'm trying to recreate those scenes in my mind, just because it looks cool.

"What was that for?" I ask, disoriented.

"Don't act as if you're in denial, Chiu."

I absolutely loathe people who call me by my last name.

"I don't know what you are talking about, Ryan. I don't want any trouble." I actually know exactly what he's referring to.

"Seriously, you don't know what I'm talking about?" Ryan seems intimidating. "Let's take it to the bathroom, shall we?" He ear drags me to the men's changing room, and I basically look like a sea lion by now.

Because he's been ear dragged so many times, he's pulling a Mr. Sadlowski move on me to retaliate. He knows this classic move all too well.

Ryan feels superior for the first time. Congratulations, Ryan.

As I'm pulled harshly towards the changing room, I notice Talinda standing by the booth, just casually watching me cleaning the gym floor. She's even eating Mom's oatmeal cookies!

"Geez, dude. Why do you have to be so heavy?" Ryan whines as he thrusts open the bathroom door. Eventually he lets go of me, and although I'm not out of shape, I'm lying down on the atrocious tile floor. Now I'm a blobfish. The school swim team, nicknamed the "Singapore Sharks," probably just had their practice session because the floor feels wet and the air feels humid.

Ryan clings to my neck with his mightiest force. He manages a death grip near the very sensitive pressure point of the male gender, the Adam's apple. That's when I know that kid is up to no good.

I wish I got some taekwondo lessons before this episode.

Forget Archie. Where is Mr. Sadlowski when you need him? Or for that matter, any of the adults in the entire school?

The kid's got his fist clenched, about to punch me with a force that could possibly knock me over. "Kid, you've got one last chance."

"One last chance," the accent resonates in my brain. I already know what had transpired beforehand. Archie discussed this matter earlier.

I remember Talinda.

Talinda.

I want to spit it all out. All out. I want to spill the beans. My mind bursts with ugly and unwanted thoughts. And I can't stand the terror on Ryan's ugly face anymore. We have been staring at each other for six stone cold seconds now.

In any case, I don't even know what would make Ryan back off. Does he want me simply to admit that I kissed his sister? Rather, does he want me to apologize for the incident? If an apology is in the cards, is it a locker room discussion or something that is more public?

And why wasn't this brought up during Summit? I suppose his anger festered for all this time. He would have been found out if he sought revenge directly during Summit.

Does it matter that Talinda egged me on to do it?

But I don't want to mention her name.

I have to do it, however.

"Uh . . . Eh . . . Erm . . . Tal . . . Talin . . . Talinda?" I try to seem unsure to Ryan, stuttering.

Ryan stares at me for another two long seconds and then—

He slaps me, leaving a scarlet red mark on my cheek with his hand imprint probably visible. "You worthless lowlife. I can't believe it. I just can't believe you kissed my sister, especially without my consent."

I don't really feel any remorse. As far as I know, Talinda has kissed a bunch of boys before. "What's the big deal?" I ask. "She's been pecking people since the sixth grade."

"No, she hasn't," Ryan denies, shaking his head with his teeth clenched.

"Yes, she has. Remember that kid Zachary MacGregor? I think he still studies here, yeah. He and Talinda sneaked into the band room once."

No response. Kids like Ryan can't afford to be criticized.

I wish I had the guts to fight Ryan. Knock him crazy with one jab in the gut and then one uppercut to the chin. And walk back out to my first PTC session.

Unfortunately, that could only happen in the Japanese cartoon series, Naruto, and I'm not Naruto.

It's also not worth getting into that much trouble.

Still, I refuse to apologize to Ryan.

Oddly, he relents. He just grunts and storms out of the boys' changing room. He seems to turn a blind eye to everything I say now. Perhaps he's going to track down Zachary MacGregor.

Else, I've been saved by the next timing for a PTC session.

From what I've been noticing lately, bullies seem to intimidate kids for no specific reason. This has been Ryan all along. He really had no motive when he hurled spaghetti and canned peaches at Horace or caused trouble on Summit. It was just plain despicable of him.

Ryan and Talinda may have the same last name, but they look totally different. Ryan must have been held back a year or two because he looks much older than Talinda. They must take after different parents. Korean parents say first-born sons take after their mothers.

After 15 minutes of hiding in the changing room, crying and feeling sorry for myself, I rise from the wet floor, dab my slap mark, wash up as best I can, knowing that all of the red marks on my face would remain. I stretch my back and exit the bathroom. I have to look at least somewhat kempt for PTCs. Hopefully I can remove that ugly image of Ryan in my head, too.

Short of kicking my right shoe onto the wall above the hand dryer, I could not do anything about that water spot on my pants bottom. That image would be a Snapchat hit.

Fortunately, I am wearing dark pants.

"What happened to your face?" Dad asks immediately after I sit down next to him.

At this time, this elevator is crowded, as dozens of parents and students assemble for the PTCs. A sign above the bank of elevator buttons reads: Maximum Capacity: 8 persons.

Clearly we're disobeying a rule in here. I'm sandwiched against a chubby kid and his two parents—triple-decker style. Mom and Dad are here as well. Mom had held my hand snugly but had to release when the doors shut.

Two of my sisters are also in the mix. We usually can't take the elevator on school days but during the PTCs an exception is made.

This crowded elevator resembles my convoluted and twisted mind. I'm in my head too much. Awkward bodies shifting around. Arms coming in contact with other arms. Scratching heads as the air circulation in the elevator is lacking.

Best to take a deep breath and hold it as long as possible.

Dad even tries to start a conversation with another family, but I just stand still. "Are you looking forward to the parent-teacher conferences?" he asks the other family.

"Who actually cares?" I say to myself.

They don't respond, although the mother offers a weak smile in return. Thank goodness I don't recognize the other clan. The father figure can't wait to alight the elevator. But that's okay. Perhaps that indicates Dad should hush.

As the whole family enters the gym, Mom says: "The decor around here is nice."

"Yeah, it really is," I reply.

"Looks the same as last semester," Sister2 offers. "I don't miss Middle School."

"Savannah, do you have any friends here whom you want to meet?" Dad asks. He always misjudges me, thinking that I have a lot of friends, despite my introverted personality. Other than maybe my roommate from Summit, I don't have anyone else to name. Every time he says that, my stomach turns. If only he knew—

"No, it's alright," I respond. I don't want to speak the truth because I'm afraid it will cause my parents a lot of grief.

My first slot for parent-teacher conferences is with my Language Arts teacher, Mrs. Harper. Not exactly doing so well in her class, so I'll see how it goes.

"Oh look, she's not conferencing anyone. Let's see her now and get this over with," I say. Mrs. Harper is munching on her favorite biscuits, looking bored to death.

"Hello there, Savannah. Nice to meet you, Mr. Dixon, Mrs. Dixon. Take a seat, you three," she says assertively. I don't think she even cares to know my parents' names, much less shake our hands.

Mrs. Harper is intimidating. I know that for a fact—her demeanor never deviates from serious. I don't think she looks to form relationships with students she teaches outside of the classroom.

I remember seeing her browse through the Women's Jeans section in Forever 21 the other day, with her earphones plugged in. Mom wore a green blouse that day and Mrs. Harper coincidentally wore a green blouse, so I almost tapped her shoulder thinking she was Mom. Thank goodness I held back at the last second. I didn't even care to say hello to her. I U-turned and immediately bolted down the aisle.

Brownie points not available. Not now, not ever.

"Ahem," she coughs, scouring for my previous Language Arts and writing tests in her strictly organized blue and yellow folders. She has to exaggerate that annoying action when teachers lick their thumbs to flip through pages. I hate that.

Mom goes straight to the point: "Is my daughter doing well in class?"

A loaded question.

My egg omelet and waffle breakfast does a somersault in my belly. Oh no. One of those odd bodily movements. What's going to happen now?

"Well, Samanth—sorry Savannah—" Mrs. Harper stutters, and then pauses.

That's it. That's when I'm almost sure that she's going to say at least one thing bad about me. Right in front of my parents. During the very first PTC of the year.

What's more, she's going to give me a lengthy lecture about how I should tighten up my grammar, and that I have lots of potential, but I don't live up to it because I'm too distracted with other commitments, such as photography and other stuff.

I enjoy photography because it allows me to express myself. I never acquired the knack of drawing or painting so I somehow eased into taking photos. As I'm not a people person, I focus on architecture and occasional street scenes. I don't have the gumption to do hardcore street photography, going up to strangers like that Humans of New York dude. Not yet, at least.

"Let's take a moment to read some of Savannah's writing." Mrs. Harper is intense and intimidating. She eventually pulls out one of my writing pieces based on a prompt: "The Haunted House."

The Haunted House

By Savannah Dixon

A foreboding, seemingly abandoned, house towered over the dead forest. Not a single tree bore life, not even parasites. A darkening night sky encroached upon the dilapidated, wooden structure. Shimmers of light shone through a foggy window on the third floor.

Though it seemed that life never existed in this place, I could sense that surreal feeling of anguished sounds of humans projecting everywhere. Drops of humidity on the barren walls descended downwards toward the floor. A creaky sound reverberated, echoing back and forth within the whole house. I entered a room of total darkness, extremely curious but mostly terrified. Long neglected, the bannisters of the staircase, or what was left of it, only held up cobwebs.

Suddenly, the only light source flickered back and forth, much like lightning. "What could that be?" I whispered, steadily crawling up the stairs to take a peek. "Someone must be in there."

The deep ringing of the house clock signaled that midnight had struck. I had no idea what was in store for me.

I wrote this at the beginning of the year, but reading every single word in it gives me a dose of shivers. I can paint a mental picture in my mind that's vivid and scary. To date, Mrs. Harper still hasn't given me a grade for this. The sad thing is: I think this was the best piece of writing I ever turned in to any teacher, in my opinion. I wonder what feedback she's going to give me now.

"You know, something that I enjoy doing with every student I conference is to talk about what they feel are their strengths and weaknesses. In class, I had the students fill out a form explaining these."

Oh, phew, I thought to myself.

"So Savannah, could you tell your parents and I what we can see from this form?"

My mind drifts off as ADHD (Attention Deficit Hyperactivity Disorder) kicks in. Soon enough, I twist my head around like an owl, except not full 360 degrees.

I notice Talinda standing next to the Booster Club booth. She seems to be looking at something. I then adjust my eyes to the subject: it's Ryan and Dominic.

"Savannah? Hello?"

I'm panicking. I've always panicked about things to myself, but rarely in front of people. That's because I've always been good at keeping things to myself. Self-inclination won't work this time.

Ryan is pulling on Dominic's ear, dragging him across the floor. This is reminiscent of the time when Mr. Sadlowski ear dragged Ryan for taunting Horace. That was a scene.

Yet again, my mind flashes back to the day my video became viral within a short time span. I remember everything—from those girls taunting me, to that large crowd surrounding me. And then my mind clicks when I think about Ryan's reaction to the video.

"Savannah," Mrs. Harper utters. Mom and Dad are nudging me by now.

My mind is juggling balls of fire as I shift my eyes between Ryan and Talinda. Ryan and Talinda. Dominic and Ryan.

Dominic kissed Ryan's sister. No, let's put it this way: Dominic kissed the school bully's sister.

And I videoed it. Even worse, I placed it on YouTube for the whole world to see. How utterly and disgustingly dumb of me, to upload a kissing video to YouTube of Dominic kissing the school bully's sister.

By the looks of this, Dominic is obviously going to get into some big, big trouble, but what about me? Am I equally in trouble for videotaping this?

Is there a word for this?

Dominic is facing the wrath of Ryan at this very minute. At the same time, Talinda is stuffing her face.

Ironically, Dominic was assigned to the same hotel room as Ryan on the raucous Summit trip.

I foretold this very moment before. This is where the real stuff happens.

Chapter 14
The Inquisition

I've already whizzed past PTCs. Nothing much there. The real stuff commences now.

My appointment with Mr. Sadlowski is scheduled for 10:30 a.m. sharp. Shoot. It's 10:25. I can't afford to miss this appointment or that would give him another reason to shoot me a long, black face. In any event, that's his normal look to students like me.

"Don't you dare do something like this again. What was going on in your mind?" Mom asks as we head up the staircase. She is worried and furious. She's not done with me; she's going to reprimand me at home later on. Let's hope she doesn't bring out the ruler.

Singaporeans have a thing with caning as a proper punishment for those who transgress the law. It has long been banned in the western world and probably in most developing countries, but for some reason, the powers that be in Singapore have decided to retain it.

In terms of pain, it varies. In third grade, my teacher slammed a plastic ruler on my back so hard that it broke in half. In that case, it's up there with ear dragging.

Caning is a means to deter serious crime. There are no rules against rulers—whether plastic, wooden or metallic.

"Is there something I should know?" Erin purrs right next to my ear.

"Nope," I respond, not amused.

"Yeah, right" she replies.

Whatever happens in that changing room stays in the changing room, I think to myself. I cannot confide in my parents or Erin. Actually, telling Erin would ensure one thing—broadcasting the episode to the entire school.

She doesn't need YouTube to be viral.

And Archie? I guess I can trust him, but he was the one who pressed me to kiss Talinda. He was vigilant in his pursuit of me on Skype. To this day, he has yet to kiss a counterpart. I suspect that would never happen for him—at least until high school. At least not until this autumn.

Talinda, who also coaxed me as well, probably knows of the fight by now. She didn't do anything to assist the situation whatsoever. To me, now I think she is equally culpable as her problematic brother.

So much for a girlfriend—if she ever was one at that. Recall Zachary MacGregor.

Our family finally makes our way to Mr. Sadlowski's office, which is Room 607. Mrs. Sadlowski ushers us through the entry of the administration offices towards her husband's office.

"Nice to see you guys today. Please take a seat," Mr. Sadlowski attempts an ingenuine smile and prepares his shots of espresso as the whole family enters the room. He has no intention of sharing his brew.

This place seems familiar. All too familiar. The place that I was introduced to directly after I kissed Talinda. This is the second time I entered this room, and that's twice too many.

Come to think of it, I had not previously been to the administration offices. I suppose I was a good student in that respect for so many years.

I'm expecting Mr. Sadlowski to say: "Please allow me to introduce you to this room," but instead, he reaches out for a handshake and begins a conversation with Erin. "Hey! Nice to see you." He's got a firm death grip, and I can tell that by the sour look on Erin's face.

"Hey," Erin responds in her innocent Bambi voice.

"How's ninth grade going for you?" Mr. Sadlowski asks.

"It's going fine. Nothing much. Just a bit harder than Middle School, but overall, just fine. No matter how hard it gets, you just have to put in the work."

"Good answer, good answer."

I think Mr. Sadlowski has intimidated us so much that we still haven't taken a seat by now.

There are only two seats and four of us standing here.

"Now tell me, Erin Chiu, are you aware at all about this situation that your brother is in right now?"

"Yes, in fact, I am," Erin stutters.

I don't even know why she is here with us.

Oddly, it appears as if Mr. Sadlowski's left eye eyeballs Mom and his right eye eyeballs Dad. He's temporarily wall-eyed. Both Mom and Dad nod their heads in approval.

"Good. Now, Erin, have there been any incidents up in the High School to your knowledge, such as PDA or anything like that?"

Erin chuckles spontaneously: "Ha, yes. Of course."

"Oh, really?" Mr. Sadlowski seems astonished, but my guess is he already knows this stuff, for a fact. "In that case, two of you might sit down. This will take some time."

Mom and I have a seat.

"Yes, really. Well, for instance, I've expressed forms of PDA before."

No. Erin. You did not just say that. You are the dumbest person in the entire world. Now, Sheriff Sadlowski thinks it's genetic, or a family tradition.

Mr. Sadlowski is even more intrigued right now. He's stoked out of his mind to let a high-schooler just let loose about her love life. It's a jackpot for the assistant principal. But Erin is just playing with real fire.

I shut my eyes and pretend not to hear any of this.

"Well, I've kissed a guy that I was dating earlier this year at school. Nobody really cared; in high school, people do it all the time."

Taking into account that Erin has dated five boys (none whom she looked good with), Mr. Sadlowski could deduce that she is just another foolish person. She's the archetype of a not-so-serious student.

When it comes to dating Erin, boys are only allowed a free trial of one month. Those who wish to continue a relationship with Erin must play a quick game of Truth or Dare. I've noticed a pattern—Erin always seems to win the game with her signature final dare—putting lipstick on the guy, taking a picture of him and uploading it to Twitter, or better yet, Snapchat. I wonder if she has done that to her current BF.

Time out. Does it really count as five relationships if three of them lasted no longer than a month?

"Stop it," I whisper, humiliated. I roll my eyes—a gesture that only Sheriff Sadlowski sees. For one, I made the fatal mistake of not objecting to my parents that Erin should also enter this fateful discussion of my academic future.

"Wait, hold up. Erin, you never told your parents that," Mom says.

Neither Erin nor I have the wherewithal to admit to our parents our wrongdoings immediately after they take place.

Mr. Sadlowski laughs raucously.

"Well—I," Erin stammers.

"You're going to be in such big trouble when we go home," Dad warns.

"Stop whatever you're doing, now," Mom chimes in. "No more boys."

Hey, wait. Didn't Mom discuss her five mottos with Erin beforehand? Again, what is this double standard? Why didn't "NO BOYS" pertain to Erin before?

Mr. Sadlowski can't take the cacophony of family banter in his exquisite room that's meant to be peaceful. "Hey, guys, I'm going to ask all of you to stop talking."

"Sorry about that," Dad apologizes.

Now with his eyes trained on his computer monitor, Mr. Sadlowski searches through his Inbox like a detective, trying to find that e-mail that he sent me, cc'ing Mom and Dad. "I just can't believe the rascals I have to deal with these days," he complains, glancing back and forth. "At first, I thought my only priority was to deal with your son, who kissed this other girl whose name I do not know. In fact, I've got a stack of cases to deal with."

Dad looks at me severely on this issue. He clearly wants me to release the name of my partner in crime. Ryan's image of terrorizing me in the boys' changing room races in my mind. And the horrendous experience of witnessing Ryan lighting fires, pouring Sprite on Horace's pillow, urinating on David's pillow.

I really want to reveal the true transgressions, but I don't because I'm not able to do so.

I relent on one subject, however.

"Talinda is her name," I affirm. "Talinda Chang."

"Yeah, whatever," Mr. Sadlowski says. "Anyways, this whole 'kissing incident' was apparently the first expressed form of PDA in our Middle School, or so I recall. Alright, pretty big deal. Then, big sister Erin barges in talking about how she committed some PDA up in the high school! And I didn't even have to ask her! How's that, huh? How messed up is that?" he rambles and rambles on and on, finding it hard to focus on finding an e-mail.

I can't believe I'm here.

"Found it!" he exclaims. "Found that e-mail. Bingo."

"Yes?" I say.

"Wow, you seem very mature in your writing skills, Dominic," he scans through the e-mail, and then reaches over the meter-long table to pat me on the shoulder. Don't know if that's emulating some kind of Polish etiquette or something.

"Ha, I love this line: 'I wish to bring back some normalcy to my reputation after this incident.' I just think that is so funny."

"Why?" I ask.

"Because it sounds so eloquent. It sounds as if you are a totally different person. Which you are clearly, inevitably trying to be right now."

"I am," I sheepishly offer. "I want to be a different person. That's the right thing to do." I try not to look at my parents when I say this. Looking at Erin, I would probably burst out laughing. She's shell-shocked, as if she walked into a minefield.

He chuckles sarcastically a little more: "You really think it's that easy? Do you?"

I turn to look at Mom and Dad.

"Do you guys think I can bring some–some normalcy back to my character?" I ask. I didn't know—until now—that the word "normal" has an extra noun derivative. What happened to "normality?" I've heard of abnormality, but what about abnormalcy?

Dad obviously nods affirmatively.

Mom agrees as well, but is puzzled at the overall situation, especially after the debacle involving Erin's confessions.

Erin just shrugs.

Dad makes sure that Mr. Sadlowski will surely agree with everything he says about me being a good student.

"I assure you," Dad begins. "That Dominic, from now on, will act in the best way that he can. He promises. Isn't that right, Dominic?"

"Yes," I affirm.

"Shouldn't that be coming from Dominic?" Mr. Sadlowski asks. "I mean, he's the one getting into this trouble."

What, is this some kind of Pledge of Allegiance? "Okay," I agree. "Here goes: I assure you, that—"

Mr. Sadlowski interrupts disrespectfully: "Dominic, nah, all of you. Why don't all of you put up your right hand and say the words out loud, again, all of you."

All of us raise our right hand and look up. For Erin, that's an arduous task because she's camouflaging her iPhone with the black desk. Oh, no. She's checking Snapchat under the tabletop to find out whether anyone checked out her recent selfie. Any other kid would be offline, at least during the last few minutes. She's unstoppable, relentless, ever so oblivious.

I nudge her, without saying anything, signaling her to put away the iPhone because what's about to happen also pertains to her.

I can't believe I'm raising my right hand in front of Mr. Sadlowski like that. Who does he think he is? That's the kind of action my parents had to do when documenting my details for applying for a new passport at the American Embassy. I was born in Singapore.

Mr. Sadlowski waves towards his office's window, directing our undivided attention to his wife, Andrea Sadlowski, who will serve as a witness. Do they get away with this all the time?

"Turn your faces back here," he roars. Mrs. Sadlowski turns around to the window to check out the scene.

"Now, repeat after me: This is a vow."

"This is a vow," all of us say.

"Otherwise a solemn promise."

"Otherwise a solemn promise." Isn't he just repeating what is said in the dictionary?

"According to Rule 102 of the Singapore International School Student Handbook—"

"According to Rule 102 of the Singapore International School Student Handbook—"

"I will not express any forms of Public Displays of Affection."

"I will not express any forms of Public Displays of Affection."

"That includes kissing."

"That includes kissing."

"Hugging."

"Hugging."

"Holding hands."

"Holding hands."

"Love bites."

"Love bites." The hell? An earlier generation called them hickeys. Gone a little too far there. It's clear he is deviating from the text. But then again, he's clearly in charge here.

"Or anything of the like."

"Or anything of the like."

"If caught for any of the above."

"If caught for any of the above—"

"I will face suspension, or in extreme cases, expulsion."

"I—will—face suspension, or in—in extreme cases—expulsion." That word makes me want to barf.

"Okay. You're done," Mr. Sadlowski says as Mrs. Sadlowski grins outside the window. "Now, you're dismissed. I've got some stuff to do."

"But aren't you going to talk to Talinda, too?" I complain. "It's only fair."

"I'm going to talk to her, soon," he promises. But who knows? He's always biased towards the girls in our school. "Now go back to your PTCs."

The four of us exit the room, subservient to his command.

I get embarrassed a lot, and I'm really good at it. This was probably the most embarrassing predicament of my life, magnified ten-fold. But why should I be embarrassed to such a self-serving assistant principal who's got nothing better to do than to exaggerate situations and ridicule his students, not to mention entire families? I sometimes wonder why we deserve to be treated this way.

"Well, for now, I'll be under Sheriff Sadlowski's watchful eye for the rest of the semester," I say.

"Thank goodness, it's the last semester of middle school for you," Dad says.

"It's kind of surreal that you're going to be in high school next year. I wonder what that would be like," Erin put a word in.

I arrive home later that afternoon, opening my computer straight away. I know exactly what I want to get accomplished by the end of the evening.

But that isn't the most important issue right now. Everybody knows about the infamous incident. Bodacious18's video has gone viral. She may have deleted it or not. It doesn't change a thing. And then there's Ryan, who slapped me for kissing his sister. There's nothing I can do about it now.

I exit all applications, other than Skype. I've figured that it's high time to split with Talinda.

Surprisingly enough, Talinda is online. She hasn't blocked me. I haven't blocked her. What?

Isn't it weird that two teenage students can kiss and within days, decide whether to block one another on social media sites?

Trusting my own instinct, I conjure up a respectful message to send that would officially end our relationship. Not that our relationship was declared official on Facebook in the first place. That would have been catastrophic.

But seriously, making a relationship Facebook official is super cringe.

"Dear Talinda," I write on Skype chat, but I don't want this to sound like an e-mail. I wish that I could have a chance to break up with her in person, but that will never happen.

I want to say a million things to her. Keeping it short and sweet would be a better option, however.

"While we may not have made this official in the past few days ever since our last encounter," I type.

[Delete]

"Hi" is all I can muster.

Talinda is typing—

She types "Hey."

Our last encounter? Should I just say what it actually was?

Oddly, I retype it again. For some reason I know that the counterparty cannot see what I type; however, in this case, Talinda sees this message for the longest time: "Dominic is typing—"

"While we may not have made this official in the past few days ever since our kiss, I just want to come to terms with you that we should bring our relationship to an end."

That sounded a bit OTT. Not at all succinct. But I don't really have time for this. I keep my eyes tightly shut as I press "enter," hearing the familiar "doot" Skype sound.

Tal replies seconds later:

"What relationship?"

Frigid wind in the tropics.

I keep my mind set on that horrific scene I just witnessed earlier today. I probably won't sleep well tonight. I suffer from mild insomnia, and it's bad enough. My body temperature shoots up every time before I go to bed, which is confusing because I don't really take hot baths or anything like that to relax.

But this incident will keep me up for days.

I am infamous. I am a notorious culprit who is solely responsible for that incident. Just think about it. If I hadn't videoed that incident, no student would have known, except Archie and me.

I am not even sure if Mr. Sadlowski had seen the kiss but for my YouTube video.

And if either Dominic or Talinda were dumb enough themselves to spread the word, they would have told confidants who probably could keep their word to be discreet. Even if friends spread the word, they could deny it ever happened.

I feel like an undercover cop who almost failed her assignment because she's just too much of a narc. It's one thing to snare seasoned criminals but it's another thing to entrap the innocent. Kissing is not a misdemeanor, much less a felony crime.

Both Dominic and I should have cleared the PTCs with ease, as in previous semesters. Having seen Dominic and Ryan in that scuffle near the men's changing room was like a double whammy. I reckon he missed one or two PTC sessions. Students are required to attend PTCs, as some teachers require students to do self-analysis of their work in the previous semester. I wonder how Dominic will make up for that.

Surely, Dominic's teachers would have docked him with some demerits going forward. Dominic's parents will be in for a surprise once the report cards are out.

In the opposite extreme, Talinda seemed aloof through the entire episode of her brother haranguing Dominic. Who knows what else happened in there? She escaped scot-free.

Chapter 15

Normalcy Shall Resume

I'm working that Monday grudge again. Same ol' routine: when the 6:00 a.m. alarm goes off, I press the snooze button and go back to sleep for another two minutes.

I should really move my alarm to a different place, so I would have to walk over there to turn it off.

By the time I roll out of bed, I feign sleepwalking over to the bathroom to brush my teeth and wash my face.

Once I squeezed face wash onto my toothbrush. Not a good scene.

Though I despise school uniforms, I am benefitted by the lack of a need to decide what to wear: it's either dark blue (now faded) or white (a bit raggedly).

Pudgy notices me eating Fruit Loops during breakfast and he begs me nonstop for a few tidbits. He lops his front paws on my lap from under the table. We tried to send him to obedience school but he failed miserably. Neutering the poor puppy helped for a few days but somehow his spirited fervor originates from his brain, not downstairs.

I use my hand to shoo him away. He knows that dogs aren't allowed to eat human food. But he doesn't need to distinguish dog food from human food.

I think Pudgy is in this dispirited state of being as of now. He mutters that familiar dog sound, which makes me feel sorry for him.

I used to call Pudgy "Fruit Loops" when I was about nine because he was such a sweet puppy. Now, he's a massive fur shedder, but still a lovable mixed breed collie. I'm a bit too old to call him "Fruit Loops" anymore.

Mom is unusually reserved at breakfast time. I don't recall the last time she actually sat down for breakfast with the family. She has an odd habit of serving everyone before she takes a seat. I reckon she's up early snacking before the household awakens.

After breakfast, I make a dash for the front door, grabbing my backpack as I make my way out.

"Goodbye, Mom," I say, as the door shuts behind me.

At exactly 10:14 a.m., recess is ending soon. I'm standing next to my locker, pretending I'm preoccupied with my own matters. So far, this day has consisted of mostly dodging Mr. Sadlowski. None of my school subjects matter.

I don't think it's worth my time to search for "Bodacious18" for now. None of that is worth my time. All I need to focus on now is just rebuilding friendships and getting my way through the hardships of eighth grade with "no more surprises," quoting Dad.

He hates surprises. Again, no news is the goal.

I hate them, too.

"Could you please move your locker door?" Tammy Moodley says in a slightly haughty voice. Perhaps I should call her Tammy Moody from now on. Many people say her expressions are exaggerated.

"No," I reply.

Moody, grabbing her snacks on the bottom locker, nudges my legs repeatedly. "Just move the locker door so I don't bang my head on it when I stand up!"

"Fine." I shut the locker door like a bad cymbal crash. "BOOM!" That's like how Dad, when playing golf the other day, grounded his driver on the tee box when his drive sliced and flirted with a water hazard to the right side. His face turned purple as his club shaft snapped in half.

I even forget to lock the locker. A trio of seventh grade girls stares at me as if I'm weird for slamming the locker door and leaving the padlock amiss. Moody will have a field day ransacking my belongings.

I stroll into math class, to find Mr. Hensley supervising the gamers during break time. Meet the lineup: Riley Smith, Ed Cho, Tess Chase, and last but not least, Horace Han.

"Time to pack up, kids. Stop gaming. It's class time," Mr. Hensley utters. Nobody knows why he's the only teacher in the school who allows gaming during recess, though it contradicts rule 89 in the Student Handbook.

He must be an elite gamer himself.

As a flood of students enter the classroom, Mr. Hensley marks the words: "Grade 9 Math Placement Recommendations" on the whiteboard.

Oh no.

These students have just come back from Math Olympiad, a contest for the most aspiring of math students in our grade. I declined to join this year because of pure laziness. Plus, I've heard from my classmates that Math Olympiad is competitive and cutthroat. If students score 60% (3 of 5 questions correct) or worse, the more successful students would mock them.

That's how messed up the system is.

I actually participated in Math Olympiad from third to fifth grade because it was easier at that time.

Whereas the primary Math Olympiads skipped class to take the exams, Middle Schoolers are required to forsake precious breaks or lunchtime for the exams. Now, that's a no go.

"Sit in your regular groups, guys," Mr. Hensley acts stern. "We are about to go over something very serious today."

"Ooohs" and "Aaahs" reverberate around the classroom.

"As we approach the beginning of March, now is the time for you lot to start thinking about math placement next year." Mr. Hensley enjoys using "you lot" because he is from Glasgow.

"Now, the Math Department here at Singapore International School has worked tirelessly to assess every student in the eighth grade in terms of math skills and achievements. Our goal is to ensure you are placed in the right class for which you are qualified. Up in the high school, there are four courses available to you: Algebra, Honors Algebra, Geometry and Honors Geometry."

Mr. Hensley then projects a flowchart on the visualizer that determines what paths students take as they go through high school.

All I can see on that chart are a bunch of APs and Calcs and other weird branches of study.

Riley is the only person sitting at my table right now. The one other guy missing is Horace Han. Oh wait. He's sitting on the classroom couch, when he's not supposed to. In T-minus three seconds, Mr. Hensley is going to blow up like a cherry bomb.

And yes he does: "Horace, get back to your seat."

Pause.

"Now!"

There we go.

Riley edges closer to me and prompts: "Hey, how's it going with you and Tal?"

I don't want to hear it.

I have two options:

1) Shove my gargantuan hand at his face, implying him to "talk to the hand," or

2) Blow up in front of the class.

I can hear five people sneering at me behind my back. While I may not be omnipotent or someone with eyes at the back of my head, I know that I am a subject of derision. Blowing up would actually not bode well with the class. But sometimes, Busybody Riley can be more irritating, more stomach churning, more downright infuriating than even Ryan.

Well, maybe not.

All I can say are the words: "You're grinding my gears. Shut up." I've hardly said "Shut up" in my life, other than to Pudgy. He reacts instantaneously over those piercing words. I think I might have said those words to Erin too, which was met with anger transcending in and out of the house throughout the whole family. I would think that because I'm the younger sibling, my parents would show more sympathy towards me. Nope.

Riley's bobbly head turns towards Mr. Hensley, then me, then Mr. Hensley and back to me. But then, I notice:

- Tammy Moody, sitting at the table left of mine with her jaw open,
- Allison Sparks, a popular redhead girl who somehow got into this honors math class mimicking Tammy,
- Horace Han doing the Horace Han, and
- Riley about to explode in hilarious laughter, else implode by holding back too long.

As I am sitting down, the diminutive Mr. Hensley somehow becomes the Eiffel Tower, standing vertical above my face so I can see his every pore on his chin. "Mr. Chiu?" His expression is daunting.

He takes a big sniff of air, his red hair and mustache ever imposing. "Could you please repeat what was said just now regarding Honors classes in a student's junior year?"

"Do I just sit here, or—?"

"No. No. You need to take your butt off of your chair and politely go up to the front to present."

Oh. I make a face that says: "I'm down with that" and head up towards the whiteboard. Frankly, I thought the buttocks comment was inappropriate.

Why doesn't Mr. Busybody (a/k/a Riley) have to go up there? Is it always my fault? Is it?

Up in the front of the classroom lies a five-inch tall wooden platform designed to meet Mr. Hensley's specifications. That's just another way of making Mr. Hensley look tall and overpowering when making lectures. On his best day with his spine straight and his chest out, he's barely 5-foot 4.

Yep, a good 5-foot 4, I repeat. Barely 5-foot 5 in clogs. Too bad he's not from Amsterdam.

I look towards the board, and then towards the students. Most of the kids glare at me like hawks; the remainder giggle like chimpanzees—minus the up-and-down arm motions and pursed lips.

"In the junior year," I begin, and then stop for another breath. "In the junior year you have the opportunity of getting into the . . . Shoot."

I fake a sneeze. The whole class pretends to feel sympathetic towards my fake sneeze.

"Out," Mr. Hensley says.

"What?"

"Out. Get out of my classroom, now."

"What, oh, okay then."

"Return to class when you feel like you are ready and fully prepared."

I don't think I deserve this. Not one single bit. Why are all odds against me? I walk out of the classroom. Riley gives me a snide smile, which I ignore.

Perhaps this is a good thing, I think to myself. Maybe, this is a time where I can contemplate about myself. I stroll around the corridor to get a breath of fresh air.

I'm just standing here, on concrete, doing absolutely nothing. I should return back to math class, apologize to my math and homeroom teacher, and then diligently listen to what the man has to say. Or I can slap Riley in the face and then become Ryan #2.

Or I can weep.

Yes, weep. I'm usually a better weeper in front of people whom I care about. I never once wept by myself. Feeling sorry for myself is something that just comes naturally to me.

Why don't I have self-control?

Why did I have to kiss Talinda?

Why did I make the first move on the dare between Archie and myself?

How did a random person surreptitiously video me, rendering things out of whack?

Why was I too scared to rat on Ryan? Surely, my actions pale in comparison to his antics.

Why does every staggering encounter with Mr. Sadlowski have to end tragically?

I lurch downstairs, still bawling a bit, to see where it leads me. I've got a long way to go.

Something odd happened tonight. While working on math homework, my sisters barged into my room, cornered me and initiated some straight talk with me.

"Savannah, I think you should reconsider your video about that Chiu kid and his squeeze," Sister1 said.

"True," Sister2 said. "It was a salacious moment in time caught on video and really, no one wins."

"Yeah, no upside all around," Baby Sis offered.

Whoa, what's this conspiracy against me? Are my sisters receiving some flak because they're related to me—the dubious Singapore International School student who cyberbullied her classmates?

I didn't really wish to discuss it with them, so I just blew them off. It didn't matter at this stage. Although I heard that Dominic got hauled into Mr. Sadistic's office not once but twice, Talinda appears to have been released scot-free.

There's a nine-month cycle to the school year. If you're still not implicated by May, you're free and clear by the end of the school year in early June. Summer vacation reigns; memories fail.

High school lurks.

On the one hand, I decry how my family does not support me in my emotional growth. I suppose that the video saga had impacted all of them, including Baby Sis who enters Middle School next year.

My sisters actually did not ask my true feelings about the subject matter. Their main concern was to provide me with guidance: delete the video.

Then again, I don't think I would have opened up with them had they wished to explore my emotions. In reality, I was depressed even before this episode. No friends, no after-school activities of note. No life.

This explains why I found myself loitering near the amphitheater on that fateful afternoon, just being abnormal.

As easy as it was to upload the video, deleting the video was even easier. No uploading delays, no processing required.

On the surface, the evidence was erased. But the damage had already been done.

MORE FISTICUFFS

Chapter 16

Revert to Reality—An Uber Kick in the Shin

Today is the six-month anniversary of the kiss, and coincidentally, the first day of high school. What if this anniversary is some kind of portent, a portent of unfortunate and ominous circumstances yet to come?

These are circumstances beyond my control.

Yesterday was new student orientation day, but all of the rising freshmen had to attend as well. I wouldn't exactly deem it a regular school day because I had permission to wake up an hour and a half later than my usual 6:00 a.m. time.

Mom cooked up a classic American breakfast with bacon, fried eggs and pancakes. That's quite dissimilar compared to the usual raisin bran gig. For the record, we only see bacon in the house once or twice a year. Mom is anti-red meat. Anti-good meat.

Come to think of it, it must've been turkey bacon.

Memories Cached

Yesterday was just another day of summer. Today being a Tuesday, the seesaw has switched sides. I feel like Garfield on a Monday again.

By the way, why does Garfield hate Mondays? He doesn't have to go to school, or work. If anything, Jon heads to work and he has a field day running around the house, rampant over Odie.

This summer has been very productive, in possibly all the wrong ways. Now my second consecutive summer of staying in Singapore, Mom flooded my desk with math and English problems. Extra tuition they call it.

Stateside, tuition strictly refers to monies paid for schooling. Tuition is another word for tutoring in these parts. You're lucky if your Mom hasn't read "Battle Hymn of the Tiger Mother," or its sequel, with a title so long that I can't be bothered to fit it in this sentence.

Seriously, it's entitled: "The Triple Package—How Three Unlikely Traits Explain the Rise and Fall of Cultural Groups in America." Whoa, the more words, the merrier. Don't forget the author is a lawyer.

Mom borrowed the book from a Korean neighbor. Oddly, Mom swears she didn't read it, yet claims she can write a better book than the Yale professor. She doesn't need to read it to make that statement. Dad raced through it for two hours and chucked it. Same review from Dad.

Isn't it ironic? Summer shouldn't have to be as monotonous as school. Then again, all of that PSAT studying will help me in my future years. But will it actually? SAT prep is on the horizon. Great.

I did get to stay up past my usual bedtime and sleep late. Going to bed at 11:00, falling asleep at midnight and getting up at 10:30 was a true highlight of the seven-week vacation. They say you grow faster while sleeping. It's a gravitational pull thing—or lack thereof.

Erin could barely survive during this time; she was forced to remain home and binge-watch movies instead of hanging out with her many friends. Many were overseas. She binge-watched 13 episodes of Pretty Little Liars' first season—all within two days. Nice.

So that concludes my rant about our unorthodox summer.

And here we go.

Freshman. Newbie. All of these are synonyms that resonate with the fact that my first year of high school is going to be a fragile one.

Legend has it that most of the seniors despise the freshmen. That's not an urban legend. I could see why that is true—imagine a flock of aliens invading your territory. Pretty frightening, right?

The truth is that seniors were once freshmen and got hazed by the upperclassmen. As such, it's the human nature side of retribution, not to mention perpetuating the tradition.

It kind of stinks that it continues in the college ranks, especially if you enter the Greek system. I hear about hazing incidents that go awry very frequently.

I roll towards the side of the bed further away from the alarm clock, using an extra pillow to drown out the clamor. Then, I curl back into a lethargic sleeping position. Fetal position is best as it prevents snoring.

Mom bellows: "Dominic. Time to wake up—it's five past six. We've got to say our morning breakfast prayer. Your sister is already changed and all set to go."

"Get over here, you little squirt, or I'll sprinkle cayenne pepper into your orange juice," Erin adds from her precipice, the peanut gallery. This summer has changed Erin for the worst.

No tolerance exists when I hear those derogatory slang words. I slam a fist onto my alarm clock and rip the bed sheets off. "That's it. I've had enough. One day, I'm gonna go ahead and rip your favorite Miley Cyrus poster into fractions."

Erin is the modern 16-year-old teenybopper.

"Do just that, and I'll throw your Green Day poster directly into a bonfire," Erin threatens. "Or Twenty One Pilots. Your choice."

"Quit bickering, you children, say your prayers and eat up your sausages and eggs before I serve you some of my leftover noodles from last night." Mom is usually oblivious to her surroundings, but not this time. She's shaking her head.

Erin rolls her eyes when mouthing her prayer.

"I can't finish these sausages, Mom," Erin complains. "I'm afraid they'll make me look chubby. You know me. I'm on a diet."

Evidently, this has dictated her stubborn attitude all along.

"Oh, is that so?" Mom replies. "That's alright, just kindly hand that over to your brother for him to eat."

"Yeah, that's alright. Might as well make him look fat. I doubt he'll get a girl anyway after his messy split with Talinda." Erin sasses impertinently, shoving her plate in my face.

"That's not cool," I respond. "And by the way, I have high metabolism."

She snatches her backpack and departs. Mom didn't even get to say: "Bye, Honeybunchee."

I say: "There's no point of being the first in line for the bus! You're going to have to sit with me anyway!"

That made her return to the house. "What do you want, you dingleberry? Hurry up!"

Mom finally gets to say: "Bye, Honeybunchees" to both of us because of me. Her superstitious thinking is as follows: that kissing both of us on the cheek and making us hug each other might just help us tackle the upcoming year.

With a small miracle—a very small one—it might just work.

Mom really does believe in small miracles.

Well, what can I say? A full school year and a full summer holiday have gone. Singapore's rising ninth graders all know what that means: eight cycles down, four more to go. At least I know I'm the only one who exaggerates.

One retiring teacher at the Middle School graduation last year pointed out that in the larger context of university years (assuming undergrad studies only and no post-grad), the graduating eight graders and their parents are just at the mid-point.

Some of my past teachers called this time the "hump" years. Although I could not agree with them more, I could not be madder at them for saying that.

Seriously, did they have to emphasize the suffering of being a middle school adolescent, namely a girl?

Puberty?

Hormones?

Studying?

Drama?

And more hormones causing additional drama?

Was that some kind of omen of things to come? I hope not.

I'd never thought school years would pass by me so quickly. Usually, I'm the type who feels that typical school days are 15 hours long and holidays collectively are 20 minutes long.

Even so, I somehow have more optimistic feelings about entering high school. I don't think that I have evolved into a different person over the course of the past seven weeks of summer break. Rather, I am hopeful that my classmates are less impulsive and certainly, less random. And I hope I can settle things with Dominic and Talinda.

Chapter 17
Sick to My Stomach

Shabby school buses screech as they circle the school roundabout. The British show "Top Gear" comes to mind.

They're dilapidated vehicles.

For a second, I imagine Jeremy Clarkson and his gang navigating the school buses in succession, never exiting the roundabout. The imagery falls apart once I realize the engines of the buses cannot pound out any real horsepower.

Though not environmentally friendly in the least bit way, the three hosts of Top Gear love to smash up and ruin what can be considered otherwise drivable vehicles. Even buildings aren't impervious to their antics. They should take on our fleet of school buses for a road rally to Malacca, Malaysia.

I dash inside the school grounds as far away from the buses as possible.

Hmm. Funny. The school administrators had the floor painted with a grey matte finish, replacing the floor that suffered from peeling paint. Another one of the many excuses to justify the outrageous tuition spike for this semester.

I sound like Mom.

An array of students, both new and returning, gather around the special peace pole in the entrance, awaiting the welcoming speech about to be given by the head principals.

Freshmen, sophomores, juniors and seniors rush around frantically, chattering away with old friends and making new ones. Quite a sight to see during this first day of school. I choose not to associate with people right now.

Keep your cool, Dominic, I say to myself.

I see a few good-looking girls left and right through my peripheral vision. In spite of being attractive, most of them are snobs that date the sports jocks.

This sophomore, named Lucy Ping, is quite the princess. Apparently she just broke up with Mitchell Williams, a standout varsity rugby player. The breakup made the rounds on Facebook over the summer break.

Ask me if I care.

I spot Archie in the distance chatting with Talinda. Let's hope they're not too chummy. Chitchat is fine ("What did you do over the break?", "What classes are you taking?"). I hope they don't delve into the infamous incident.

Archie acknowledges me, then says goodbye to Talinda. I don't even look at Talinda. He then shoves his way towards me, in his trademark obnoxious way. Suddenly, he hugs me, as if we are long lost friends. Come to think of it, we haven't talked in a while.

Archie camped out in the English countryside for most of the summer at his great aunt's retreat. He spent the summer doing what Brits do best: hunting pheasants.

"What's up, my main man?" he says in his signature British accent. He sports strong peppermint breath as well. Do they say "main man" in the UK? The boy is confused due to living in Singapore, with a school population dominated by Asians. The number of students from expat families seem to dwindle each successive year.

"You look swell. How's it going with Talinda?"

"What are you talking about?" I ask, confused. Of course he's joking.

Archie bumps my right arm with his elbow and winks.

"Well, nothing much," I say. "We haven't been talking as much lately, especially since we broke up. I'd rather not associate with her. In reality, we were never a couple. Talinda confirmed this over Skype."

"Oh, that's unfortunate."

I nod. It's just as well. Talinda actually blocked me on Skype when school ended last year.

"It was a cold move," I say.

"Frigid cold," Archie sympathizes.

"Welcome," a familiar voice bellows as a man steps up to the podium.

Wait.

He is all too familiar. It's the notorious Mr. Sadlowski.

Did he leave the Middle School in sync with me? Is he the new assistant principal for the High School?

No, this can't be happening. I slap myself in the face twice to make sure I'm not in the year 2065. I'm hoping to time warp, either to the past or to the future. Either way is fine—anything to avoid this.

Unfortunately, I'm still in the year 2015.

Now his voice is almost inaudible due to the defective microphone. The crowd giggles.

"Welcome to the 2015-16 school year, everybody!" he shouts enthusiastically, and then coughs.

The Most Irritating Noise in School must be a malfunctioning microphone accompanied by staticky loudspeakers. In this case, the ear-piercing, high-pitched Woooonnnnnngggg and smattering of electrical static cause the entire crowd to cover their respective ears and grimace.

The second worst sound in the world is fingernails scratching a chalkboard. But in this modern age, teachers have been weaned off chalkboards and now prefer whiteboards and markers.

Or projecting their laptops onto Apple TV.

Some don't even lecture any more. They just say a few words from behind their desks and then let the kids loose. The coolest teachers are the ones who show movies and play EverWing on their phones, like Mr. Freaking Hensley.

Encore: Wooonnnggg!

Every single person in the school is probably intimidated.

"Chins up, eyebrows up, everybody! This speech that I am about to share with you indicates the beginning of another successful, prosperous year. And that, my friends here at Singapore International School, means that all of you will need to work together to fulfill your duties. That means studying hard so that you can play harder. Understood?"

"Yup, sure thing," a sarcastic kid mumbles. At least the nerds and a few gunners are listening.

"Understood?" Mr. Sadlowski bellows.

"Yes!" an eighth of the audience wakes up.

"Never had I ever seen a community where so many intelligent, well-rounded, sporty, skillful kids from all different sizes, races and spiritual backgrounds congregate into one school. Throughout my decades as a teacher and principal in the Middle School and now in High School, I have never seen such a sight."

Here, he mimics a pirate perched in the crow's nest of a ship, scanning the seas for the next target. His left and right hands are cupped over his eyes as he looks from side to side.

Roughly 800 students look at each other awkwardly.

Ms. Grace Sullivan, the head principal steps up to the podium, poised, fixing the collar of her slender black suit. She takes over the mic: "May the new students and incoming freshmen and the returning students divide into two groups: one group to the left of the peace pole and one group to the right of the peace pole.

I roll my eyes. I feel sick to the stomach, knowing that I would have to undergo many more years of school before setting off for college.

"My guess is that we're going to have to do some icebreakers," Archie comments.

"Oh, great." This is like summer camp.

"Throughout the course of this school year, with each and every class each one of you take part in, you must all aim to achieve a main goal: academic excellence," Ms. Sullivan proclaims. "If you all don't strive to achieve this goal, and instead call it quits at any time, you are undercutting your future." She utilizes a multitude of hand gestures to prove her point.

Almost half the students hail from expatriate families. Most of us will attend university Stateside, else in the United Kingdom or Australia. A fair number of local students will attend Singapore's universities. I suppose she is saying that we should work harder so that we can apply for the Ivy League and the other private and state schools comprising the top 20 schools rather than community colleges.

The seniors seem relaxed but they have one final push. This is their final year of high school, and they will need to file their college applications in the coming months. A few diehards will go for early admission with the elite schools. One or two life sciences nerds will apply for a combined undergrad/medical school program in six or seven years rather than the customary eight.

"If you came to this school just for the popularity, for the fame, for the attention, you will not have a successful year." Ms. Sullivan glares at a few students just for show.

"Check that out, that's the first time we've ever heard such a thing," I remark.

"Ditto, this is becoming into a harangue," says Archie.

"Returning students, meet your new friends. Now is the time to mix and create new and abiding friendships. While academic excellence is emphasized, it isn't the only thing you should worry about. We want each and every student to have solid relationships with peers."

Social exclusion runs rampant at our school as well. If overt, I find it to be a type of bullying. There are some kids who feel like they don't belong to an otherwise strong-minded and close-knit group of students here at the Singapore International School.

It's an odd sight. The returning students surround a core of new students, including 200 freshmen and approximately 75 new students. It's as if the lead singer of the rock band wants the crowd to form a donut (circle pit) so that the hardcore guys can slam it up in the middle.

We mix in. There's no slamming.

The nerds attract the other nerds; the cool dudes attract the other cool dudes. Not really much diversity exists so far. I notice a variety of awkward facial expressions appear on kids' faces, and no one is really eager to make new friends. One or two jocks (returnees) try to mack on the handful of good-looking gals I saw earlier.

Same old jabber. Same old principals.

The popular kids and the cliques assemble into masses like the earth's convergent plates shifting together to form a new continent. The outcasts and new outsiders form Madagascar and maybe Tasmania.

Ms. Sullivan, Mr. Sadlowski and a few of the other teachers vigorously shake hands with the new students on the front fringe and of course, the standout veterans. And where can Mrs. Sadlowski be found?

Archie and I stay together and attempt to greet some of the other new geeks somehow invited into this school.

Mr. Sadlowski hops back onto the podium: "Are you guys ready for a rewarding school year?"

"Yes!"

"Absolutely!"

"Totally!"

"Of course!"

"Without a doubt!"

"Eh." That's me.

"No." That's my sidekick.

"Now come on over and head over to your designated homeroom."

Geez. I've probably had enough of that speech. I hadn't actually realized that twenty minutes of my life had just been wasted after that. Irretrievable. This talk was probably the longest twenty minutes of my entire life. To think, we might have to hear it three more times before we graduate.

Mr. Sadlowski notices me. I'm about to exhale a prolonged sigh when I notice his menacing gaze, which probably only means one thing: From this point on, he's going to be on my back, all the way until I graduate and move on to college. Mr. Sadlowski is my one and only obstacle from achieving that goal.

Mr. Sadlowski probably advanced to the high school due to his long-term commitment to the School. But how was he assigned assistant principal of the High School? Isn't the obvious progression to become principal of the Middle School?

I have no idea.

He's got the big eyes and the peripheral vision of a superior hawk. That means he can casually pretend he's gazing at someone else when he is in fact glaring at me. Every time he wears a pair of sunglasses, I find it hard to tell exactly who he's looking at.

What's more, he's got the bug eyes of someone's worst nightmare.

My worst nightmare.

How amazing it is for him to discern me amongst a crowd of rambunctious teens when I'm more than 20 meters away from the podium.

Mr. Sadlowski stares at me for an extra two seconds, and then swaggers off to the office.

At that point, I almost regurgitate my breakfast. Almost.

I would not say that I forgot about the unfortunate events of the previous year. During the summer, I would have some dreams, which turned into nightmares, about the saga. Worse yet, I would let my mind wander during the daytime hours as well.

Whereas my sisters engaged in various activities over the summer, including swimming lessons, PSAT/SAT preparation and summer camps, I tended to stay at home reading books on my Kindle.

Young Adult novels are my favorite, especially fantasy fiction. I enjoy escaping to other worlds.

Let's hope that Dominic has at least moved on about the incident, although I know that will not be possible. None of my prayers have been heard.

Here I am, disembarking my school bus. At precisely 7:30 a.m., the entire student body will find out all of their classes.

My self-esteem has dropped close to the minimum. If I don't make any friends here this year, I won't be able to succeed later in life. Ninth grade is the right time to make friends. Scratch that, it's the final time.

Mom and I had a discussion about this over the summer. It was a bit of a shock for me, as Mom usually doesn't make the time to have a mother-daughter chat. I will chalk it up to a one-off and Mom having some rare down time.

Mom thinks otherwise; she says that friends will only drag my grades down.

I often reply along the lines of: "Having friends boost self-esteem and confidence, and will therefore improve my grades."

Mom thinks I'll do fine being a loner. I wasn't always one, though. In elementary school, probably fourth or fifth grade, I had one best friend named Kelly. She had shared the same passions and pursuits as I had at the time: basketball.

Before her family moved back to California, I remember writing an e-mail, acknowledging her departure and saying that I'll miss her. I can't recall the exact words, but I know I wrote a considerably long note—longer than any essay I would have submitted to my fifth grade Language Arts teacher.

Kelly only replied with six words: "Bye, Savannah. I'll miss you too ☹."

Isn't that so sad? In a world where girls focus on petty issues over their friends and waste half an hour on a single chat session,

Kelly just replied with a dull response. I was taken aback at her lame reply. It was better than not replying at all, but was still pathetic, considering how good friends we were.

Then again, these days, kids will only respond with an emoji. If at all. Maybe I was thinking too much—overdoing it.

Suffice to say, I never heard back from Kelly ever again, though I see a few gleeful Snapchat vids of her from time to time. Oh well.

On this first day of school, I mill around the perimeter of the school grounds, far away from the cool crowd near the peace pole. In the distance, I can see Dominic and Archie. No sign of the resident bully but I think I make out Talinda as well. Ryan must be in the neighborhood. He's not the boarding school type.

The Middle School has a stellar reputation for standouts in island-wide academic competitions; however, the number of rising ninth graders is diminished by the number of students who move on to boarding school on the east coast Stateside or to the U.K. It's the main intake of students whose parents have a legacy of boarding school backgrounds, as well as the nouveau riche.

When Ms. Sullivan requests that the students separate between incoming students and returnees, I remain in the section intended for incoming students. No one cares to single me out for the mistake. I do not want to budge in the hot Singapore sun.

If I make my mark in high school, it won't be today.

Chapter 18
Suck It Up

Next to Mr. Sadlowski's office, an A3 sheet of laminated white paper containing the information about homeroom assignments is fastened on the wall. This particular sheet of paper is allocated to the freshmen. Three other similar-sized sheets are positioned in other parts of the administration offices for the sophomores, juniors and seniors.

It's a nonsensical idea. Why can't we just look up our designated classes on our webpage? That would be too easy, too organized. Or efficient.

Ah, that's right.

The administration sent out an e-mail the night before notifying us that we should not bring our computers or smartphones to school because the first day should be a technology-free, get-to-know-each-other day. In their regular stead, the gamers broke some rules today on the bus when they pulled out their laptops to play BombSquad.

As I can tell, Mr. Sadlowski probably hired a dozen professional furniture designers and maybe even a few painters because his office is completely overdone. Considering it's his first year at the high school, I'm surprised he's allowed to have such an exquisite office to himself.

"Do you guys fancy my office?"

No one says a word. I almost burst into tears on the ground laughing, but the population density in this area is too large for me to even touch the ground.

Clearly Mr. Sadlowski's egotistic mind is setting him off to his own dream world.

"Alrighty then," his ego drops a few notches. "Knock yourself out, kids, and get to your homeroom as quick as possible."

Unfortunately, the majority of the people standing here are either fat, or just another cluster of potential Yao Mings but with more girth. What's more, the font size of the text is about 10 point, forcing me to squint my eyes.

All of a sudden, the ground shakes. Somewhat vigorously. It's either a major thunderstorm or just some building structure malfunctioning.

But no, it's none of that. The improbable occurs: One of the fat kids triggers a domino effect after charging into the crowd. He collapses to the ground like a dead walrus. More than 200 pounds of blubber lies stone cold on the ground.

And one-by-one, a portion of the army falls. It's not a pretty sight.

I'm expecting Mr. Sadlowski to slingshot out of his office door, plow through the crowd and turn into a raging monster, but he doesn't. He's in his wife's office, borrowing some of her coffee beans. Both are oblivious to their surroundings.

Good news for me. Thankfully, I can see the chart more clearly.

Finding my name in that chart is an arduous ordeal. More than 200 students' names are listed in the chart, each name providing details of classes and the teachers. Because lots of students have a surname commencing with "C", I'm taking longer than ever to find my name.

I think there are roughly 50 of such people.

Yeah, 50.

After finding it, I take about ten seconds to fully digest how absolutely terrifying and horrifying my classes this year appear to me right now.

Apparently, I've been placed into the geekiest math class in the entire grade: Honors Geometry. It sounds quite intimidating and demanding.

I peer closer at the three words, slightly bewildered. Never before had honors classes existed in past grade levels. I had been in a standard regular math class in the years previous.

Since when was I eligible for an honors class? Well, aside from poor work habits from my previous year's math class, I did excel in summative exams.

But being placed in a straight-up honors class for my freshman year is a bit unnerving.

Off to the side of the laminated paper shows a starred box that says:

> **Students must maintain a B- or above in an honors class within the first quarter of the school year. Otherwise, following a discussion with the department, the student may have to drop down to a regular class.**

The bold text itself is daunting.

The good news is that I'm only placed in an honors class for math. Aside from the fact that my science class contains the exact same students as my math class, I have Religion and Photography & Digital Imaging I, both as peaceful retreats. Sadly, Archie is the only close friend I have for these chill classes. The rest are kids with whom I've never interacted with in person before, or just plain old new kids.

Unlike most of my other friends from previous years, I have stayed in the same school for seven years running now. I can't imagine being a new kid trying to make friends in unfamiliar territory.

We've all read those predictable picture books in the third grade, where the new kid starts off as an introvert, then gets bullied, and then finally makes some friends. We've all heard of that tired story.

Without a doubt, it takes me a few weeks, if not months, to get used to having a new kid around. Occasionally, the new kid becomes popular right away, hanging with all the girls and pretending he's cool.

So this year, I'll stay close to Archie the whole time. Let's just hope he doesn't buddy up with a new kid and drift away from me. If he does, I'd be tilted, but I won't be manipulative.

All I'm thinking about right now is my math class, honestly. There's really no other reason to justify why I got placed in classes with such socially inferior people.

The way I read it, Honors Math relegates me into nerd-dom. By the way, the top math class dudes—usually Korean or Indian kids—will make an annual junket trip to Miami for an international math contest and swing by Disney World before making their way back. It befuddles me that the school would subject these kids to jetlag before a math competition.

A handful of the Honors Math kids, including myself, will, for the entire academic year, pretend to be cool when all things are stacked against them.

I suppose I'll have to make some new friends to survive in that class.

So far, on this particular first day of school, I have never felt worse. My head hangs low as I approach homeroom, two floors up and light years away.

I decide to head to my locker first, which reads 1112 on the first floor—furthest away from the cafeteria. What's more, it's a bottom locker, which means the door on locker 1109 (diagonal top left from mine) will swing open and hit my head. How unlucky.

Guess I'll be holding grudge for the guy who got lucky locker 1111.

Worse yet, I'll suffer the fate of Tammy Moody.

Then again, I heard most high schoolers don't even use their lockers, opting to lug their books and laptop throughout the day. No time for a proper lunch, nor chitchatting on the way to class, much less hitting the locker every other hour.

The atmosphere around me is hectic and bustling. Old friends are getting reacquainted. Most of the incoming students are finally getting to know each other, making new friends and all.

But for me, I'm still in awe.

What does it feel like to be excited about school? You don't often come across a time when you can't sleep the night before thinking about the insanely lame classes you've been put in the next day or how your social life would be crushed throughout the coming months.

In high school, you either focus and buckle down on studying, or goof around with friends until you barely graduate. Each has its pros and cons. There is no middle ground. It only gets tougher, not easier.

Again, I sound like Mom.

I pass by a noticeably humongous library on the fourth floor, and through the glass window, I see a number of assorted couches and beanbags.

I glance at the clock.

It's now 8:06. Four minutes until homeroom.

The thought lingers in my head, making me want to sleep in one of those couches nonstop until someone wakes me up for college.

However, there's no stopping now. I'm beginning to experience my own angst just walking into homeroom.

The angst of anticipating what kind of stress, anxiety and drama that will arise during this coming school year.

The angst of girls.

The angst of maintaining good impressions on your teachers.

The angst of hardcore drill-sergeant studying.

The angst of the PSAT, the cousin to the dreaded SAT. Not to mention AP exams, college applications and essays, and all of that hubbub.

Don't forget: Be Disciplined and No Girls.

As I come close to homeroom, I am mindful that all of the above will begin in T-minus one second.

Word spreads soon about how a chubby freshman kid employed the use of the "domino effect" outside Mr. Sadlowski's office earlier this morning. Once I found out, I thought it was pretty funny because although I hadn't seen it, I could paint a vivid video in my head. Then, I would replay the video back and forth, over and over again, like in a GIF. It would work well alongside a "Shooting Stars" track.

Wait, I'm not supposed to mention anything about a video. Otherwise, that will spread across the high school as well. I can't let the intimidating seniors know. I can't let anyone else know.

As the students all squint to read their assigned classes, the cumbersome laminated paper's right edge loses its traction against the glass pane. The stickiness of the tape probably wore out a bit too soon due to the high humidity. One edge down, three to go.

"Get some blu-tac!" Jesse Ross complains. She was the nasty girl who summoned her four sidekicks to tease me that other time. I pretend not to notice her.

Mr. Sadlowski and his wife try to calm the frantic students down. They're clearly ready to start the year strong, but I'm not.

Oh no. This is bad.

I'm assigned to three classes with Dominic and one with Talinda. With Dominic, I have Homeroom, Honors Geo and Phys Ed. I've got Humanities with Talinda. The only clear classes are Film and Media Arts and Science. Film and Media was my third choice in the sign-up sheet I filled out last year for electives.

My first and second choices were 3D Studio Art and this class called Women's Rights, respectively. That left me with the third spot blank, where I had the choice of either selecting Film and Media Arts or Drama or Musical Theater. Film was the final choice because both Drama and Musical Theater are completely ill-fitting to my personality.

Mr. Sadlowski could have easily chased me down for uploading that video last year, but he didn't. He seemed to focus more on the PDA. I dodged getting in trouble with him. I didn't get away with exposing my cyberbullying episode to the world.

Had Dominic and Talinda, or their respective parents, contacted YouTube proctors, they could have sought the removal of the video and the accompanying vindictive and asinine comments. I never understood why YouTube allows comments, especially the non-G-rated ones.

Memories Cached

I suppose to monitor comments on any popular website is cumbersome and in most cases, impossible.

As I proceed to my assigned locker: 1109, I think about a few things. Firstly, an odd-numbered locker is a top locker, which won't strain my back as much as a bottom one, where I'd have to kneel down to store a 12-pound bag. Twelve pounds is a bit much for my flimsy-shaped figure.

I don't like the fact that our computers have to be so unwieldy. Might as well stack some dumbbells in my bag.

Lockers 1100 through 1150 are all located indoors, making the surroundings very humid. The smell around here is that of white paint, suggesting refurbishment. I open my locker, praying that there won't be any hardened peanut butter stuck in a crevice, as in the case last year.

The tropics of Singapore make it even more unbearable. There are no seasons here, just variations of one theme: wet summer, dry summer and summer summer (i.e., hot).

"Hey," a distinctive voice murmurs on the other side of the hallway. His voice is in the baritone range.

It's Dominic who appears out of the corner of my eye. My skin releases a sudden jolt once I realize it's him. My mind almost pops, water balloon style.

Pretending to ignore him isn't probably the best idea now, so I just whisper a barely audible: "Hi." I then leave the locker door ajar so that it conceals his view of my face.

Quick. Think of something to do. Hiding your face won't help; it will only make things look more suspicious, I think to myself.

"Hey," I repeat myself for the second time, while slowly peeking out of the locker door.

The hallway door closes shut with a clamorous "Bang!" He's gone, without a trace. I don't know whether this was a missed opportunity or not. I feel like he intended to greet someone else. Why would he instigate this suddenly?

I breathe several sighs of relief.

Chapter 19

A Look of Reassurance

A chorus of loud juvenile greetings hounds me as I step into class. Homeroom for me this year is designated in a science lab. It's odd to have home base in a science lab. It's hard to chill in such a space, as there's not a single couch to be found. I'm definitely not used to this setup. It's a cold environment with beakers and test tubes lining the cabinets and austere lab equipment on a dozen workstations.

"Welcome to the club," Mr. Clark, my new homeroom teacher says. "And, you are?"

"Dominic Chiu."

Despite his seemingly "American" last name, he's got a somewhat strong European accent. Whatever accent it might be, he's also sporting a somewhat strong cologne as well. Of course, all that is complemented by loose jeans.

Dad jeans (a/k/a Barack Obama jeans).

"Dominic Chiu . . . hmm, let's just see," as he scans the attendance sheet for a few seconds. "Sorry, it's taking longer than ever to find you, as there are six people in this homeroom with the last name of 'C'!" he blurts, patting his desk and laughing at himself.

I offer a wry smile and analyze the other boys and girls lounging around in the classroom.

The girls chat amongst each other, gossiping about their current infatuations, while the boys are toying around with a newfound game they discovered at the end of summer break.

My quick analysis proves that the girls are anything but attractive or smart, and the boys are nothing but gamers. Eh, perhaps at least one of these guys may be intelligent. Still, I disapprove.

I grimace at the thought of having to endure the hardships of being in such a class for another year of my life. Looking into the future, I don't think things would bode well from any perspective.

A few seconds later, the "domino" kid appears through the front door. "My name's Hal Marks," he says.

I can't tell whether if he's laughing or crying about the recent incident. Probably both. Ultimately, his brain can't decide. He also can't tell whether the incident tarnished his whole reputation for the school year. Man, what a poor guy. Then again, to be oblivious is divine.

"Sorry, Teach, I'm late," he apologizes, placing his bag on one of the stools.

"It's alright. You get a one-off freebie."

What? A freebie? I never knew those really existed in high schools.

"Come take a seat over here. By the way, you can call me Mr. Clark if you'd like. It sounds better than 'Teach'."

The domino kid raises his eyebrow accompanied by an odd-looking scowl. International students in Singapore rarely come across teachers who aren't accustomed to the use of slang.

Hal must take after his father, though less punctuated.

The class giggles.

"Students, one more student has yet to arrive homeroom before we officially begin our first class," Mr. Clark strokes his beard and slouches on his chair, exposing a third of his salmon-pink, round belly.

And then lo and behold, another student rolls in late.

"Sorry, Mr. Clark, I'm late for homeroom. My name's Savannah Dixon."

I widen my eyes with complete and utter disbelief. Is Savannah Dixon actually in my homeroom? Yes, Savannah Dixon, whose code name is the infamous "Bodacious18?"

I have no clue what I'm supposed to do now. Approach her and acknowledge her presence? Reprimand her for uploading the video?

No, I can't do that in front of the whole class. Plus, I don't even know her.

After greeting Mr. Clark, she turns to my direction and almost murmurs: "Hey," but doesn't.

"Hello," I say. I suppose I went first.

Although a lab table toward the back of the room has an empty seat, Savannah takes the first seat closest to the door, which is right next to me. We're surrounded by a group of gossip girls.

I'm the type of person to hold grudges for a long time.

Clearly, there is a bit of friction between the two of us. For the next two minutes straight, neither of us dares to raise the inevitable. Most of the rest of the class must be holding back from bursting out in laughter. The irony.

"So, you're the person who uploaded the vid—"

"Yeah, that was me," Bodacious18 interrupts me so confidently.

"Yep," I say as we both droop our heads for another good ten seconds. We receive an instant reprieve by Mr. Clark excusing himself when another teacher knocks on the classroom door. "Excuse me, kids, I'll be back in a second."

I would think Savannah would bring up the point on her own, but she's too scared to say something out of the blue. I can see it in her eyes. And maybe she expects me to be sterner due to the dynamics of this perplexing situation.

We both sigh as we look into each other's eyes.

She gives me the expression as if she wants to utter something, but she's still unsure. I'm unsure as well.

Does she want to apologize? Am I supposed to forgive her from the outset?

Nah, that would be too lenient.

"Listen, Dominic. I'm sorry," she confides in me.

I pause for a moment, in a quandary over what to say next. Savannah seems like a good-natured person from the outside, although I can only say that from my ongoing face-to-face experience I've had with her.

"I am sorry. I just needed you to know." Savannah focuses her eyes on mine, hoping for an answer. "You didn't deserve the attention or infamy that you received. You shouldn't have gotten in that much trouble."

Her left hand rests on my shoulder, and I hadn't realized until now.

Nobody has ever placed a hand on my shoulder, besides Erin on a bad day or Mom on a really bad day.

I look up, exhale and finally say: "It's okay." I don't know if I was right about saying that. Somewhere in my mind tells me that was a mistake. Or not.

Still, Savannah persists: "Are you really sure?"

"Yeah, it's fine. It's fine," I mumble those words in rapid succession. I sound way too confident for the situation.

Then I say: "Listen, we don't really know each other a lot or anything right now. We should probably discuss this later sometime."

I just really needed to let that out.

Having to forgive another person after such an arduous ordeal is a most difficult task. That said, I don't think I've ever had to forgive a girl for anything. Brother-sister squabbles don't count. I'm usually more accustomed to my parents or "any other higher power" forgiving me, because I'm the one who causes trouble. Even if my parents do something wrong and I'm compelled to speak out, I don't.

From Savannah's perspective, this act of contrition is also a daunting task. No one knows the odds of us being placed in the same homeroom, much less being seated next to one another. In some ways, she's benefitting from the passage of time. The episode from last year seems ever so distant.

Savannah shoots me a look of reassurance, and that's when I know she is no longer fretting.

It's a good feeling to apologize, even if it's almost six months too late. Unfortunately, I'm still skeptical over the fact that Dominic forgave me over this grave matter. There's not really much to know on his mind when he utters a lame: "It's okay." Those two words are like a prelude for a cliffhanger. An unresolved issue.

I've never had a close relationship with another boy. As such, I am unable to decipher whether Dominic's reaction is atypical or otherwise. Do boys have shorter-term memories than girls? Are boys less vindictive than their female counterparts in these types of circumstances? Do boys forgive others more easily?

One thing I've heard is that teenage boys are less apt to express their true feelings, which carries over into manhood. Boys tend to act out when trying to impress others—either with male or female friends in tow.

The short exchange we shared in homeroom was a bit stilted, as we had to exchange our thoughts with almost two dozen other students in our midst. No doubt most of the audience was well aware of the content.

When I was young, I would fight often with my sisters—over the slightest of things, such as over toys, magic markers and such. As my parents are forever at work and busy with extra-curricular activities, the maids would be charged with disciplining the girls.

But all they would do was corral us into a circle and force us to apologize to one another. Invariably, Sister1 led the way in terms of kicking off the apologies, followed by Sister2 and so on. In the end, Baby Sis would usually get her way.

We never fought over boys.

Looking back, this is the very first time that I apologized to a boy. It was a natural thing to do, especially given my long-standing remorse.

Had I known Dominic or Talinda better, I would have apologized earlier. Way earlier. Then again, if that were the case, I probably would not have uploaded the video if we were better acquainted.

As Talinda hasn't been implicated in the fiasco with Mr. Sadlowski and everything, I suppose I don't need to apologize to her.

Or do I?

Chapter 20

Ryan

Life passes at full blast after my first introduction to this year's classes.

Hopefully, lunchtime would give me a chance to talk with my friends for half an hour. I approach Archie, who's spitting out rapid-fire French with his new teacher. The kid seems to have mastered the hardest part of the romance language: verb conjugation. Archie is very intellectual and has a photographic memory, which explains why he can fluently chat in four foreign languages—the other three are Spanish, Italian and Dutch.

I should nickname him Dutch boy.

He utters some more before noticing me standing alone.

"Comment ça va? Bloody heck, man, where have you been? Où étiez-vous?" Archie exclaims.

"I feel the exact same way, man. I guess that means we must stay closer together throughout this year. I need my wingman at all times possible."

"True that."

I grunt. I'm just a few hours into ninth grade, and my nerves are starting to fray.

No surprise that the whole grade reeks of disparity. Here, we have the nerd cliques, the cool cliques and the peripherals.

Immediately, I observe Savannah ambling towards the lunchroom serving line. She appears overwhelmed.

She's standing about three meters away, staring at the pineapple-glazed sweet and sour pork.

Every time I take one step closer to address her, she seemingly steps away. I supposed she's trained in thought about the lack of selection: what's the best of the worst?

"How are your classes stacking up for you?" I attempt to engage.

"Oh, hi, Dominic. I guess they're fine. It's going to take me a few days to get used to our new school and this new environment."

"That's cool," I cough, wiping my nose inadvertently. "Sorry, allergies."

Savannah laughs a bit, and it's the most distinctive laugh I have ever heard. She perks up her large hipster glasses.

Archie swaggers right in front of me, giving me the awkward wink that only he can muster. I return with my eyebrows and forehead frowning.

At least 20 seconds pass, and I realize I'm standing right behind Savannah in this long line with no tray. You can't be this stupid, Dominic, I whisper to myself.

"Um, Savannah, would you be so kind enough to save this spot for me? Thanks."

I turn back towards the start of the line to find a tray, and I get shoved. "Watch where you're go—?" I utter. Who did I just say that to?

Ryan.

The renowned troublemaker cracks his neck and knuckles, and broadens the Grand Canyon of his chest. From his appearance, he grew three inches in the sternum area and also shrunk a good inch in height, making him stockier than a wrestler. "You trying to hide from me, Chiu?"

"Um, no, when?"

"This morning. You congregated with your sidekick, the British kid."

I raise my eyebrows and call out: "You mean, Archie?"

Archie bounces from his seat, with ramen noodles flying in uncontrolled directions. "I heard my name."

Ryan and two kids form a gang, entourage style. New kids—Danny Lau and Kenny Thomas—are the cohorts. They both still sport name tags on their shirts.

"Is that your new boy band?" I ask.

Ryan sniggers. Maybe my joke was good.

"Nah, we call ourselves the 'Triple Threat'. Listen, Chiu, why don't you make your way to the back of the line? Better yet, skip lunch."

"Nah, I'm good." I emulate Ryan. "Savannah so kindly offered to save my spot."

"Not my problem. If you don't do as I say, I will either report you to the office for cutting or stuff you in one of those janitor lockers. How's that?"

I smirk. I could only imagine kids reporting Ryan to the office, not vice versa. Savannah burrows her head into her folded arms. Meanwhile, the fat kid who collapsed this morning giggles. He's just so glad he's not the one who's going to be forced into the claustrophobic janitor's locker.

"Listen, Ryan," I bellow. "I don't want any trouble this year with you. Just leave me and my friends alone, understood?"

"Heh, it's not going to be that easy, Chiu. I'm still holding grudge over what you did to my sister."

"Fine, I kissed her. Are you still thinking about that? Is that all you think about?" I feel frustrated.

Ryan snickers.

"You imbecile," I continue. I am unstoppable. "You urinated on David's pillow. You created a flamethrower using matches and deodorant in our bathroom. You invited harmful creatures onto Horace's pillow. What kind of monster does that?"

Ryan edges closer to me. He hasn't discovered the effectiveness of antiperspirants. His cheeks puff up to a scarlet red, arms flexed. He places a rigid index finger on my chin.

Members of the entourage have been taken aback by my short inventory of Ryan's rap sheet. Initiation, Ryan-style.

Luckily for Ryan, and by default—me—Mr. Clark saunters in the lunchroom with two other teachers. They shoot looks over in our direction.

"Oopsies," Ryan says as he relents and allows me to resume my place in line. He and his boy band face the front, hands gripping their trays ever so tightly.

He's like a totally different person with one or more teachers present. I don't think the teachers even noticed a possible bust-up.

There you have it. Whatever conclusion I drew from my chat with Dominic in homeroom class is now smashed by this episode with Ryan threatening Dominic. Before the fateful episode, Dominic and I were talking as if nothing had happened. We were super casual, and it appeared as if Dominic had completely let go of the issue.

He even initiated the conversation with me in the cafeteria. He seemed unsure at first, but carried on.

Based upon the tension between the boys and my observation that Dominic was trying to stand up to the bully and his henchmen, I am now certain that this will not be the last conflict between the boys.

And so the Ryan saga continues during official school hours.

It haunts me again. Had I not uploaded the controversial video, Ryan would not have ammunition to pick on Dominic.

Not confrontational, I didn't think to stand up for Dominic during the recent encounter in the lunchroom. In any event, what could I have said? I'm gun-shy.

Thank goodness Mr. Clark stepped into the lunchroom at that point in time.

Chapter 21
Inferiority Complex

The teenage mind, Dad believes, is the hardest one of all to understand. He can so easily tell that by the look in my eyes as we sit next to each other in the SUV. Four kilometers into our drive towards the shopping mall, neither of us have said a word yet.

Chills.

"So, Dominic, how was school this week? Any bullies?" he asks.

Ah, most parents just ask "How was school?"; whereas, Dad's new spin entails asking about the presence of bullies. It just makes me shiver.

The answer should be "yes" but I'm hesitant to admit it.

"No," I murmur instead. "No bullies." I'm hiding two crucial events that trump anything else I've experienced before: that I forgave Savannah, and that Ryan yet again instigated another bullying session, only to have been blocked by Mr. Clark's sudden presence.

Sure, I could have answered Dad's interrogation in the affirmative, but that would only plunge me deep down into a never-ending spiral of questions to come. I cannot fathom surviving that.

Dad raises one eyebrow while still keeping his eyes on the road. No words need to be spoken now as the eyebrow movement confirms my flawed response.

Saying "no" proves my inner unease.

"You know, it's kind of easy to tell when you are lying or not," Dad comments.

It's so shockingly true. My limbs don't move when I lie. Rather, I stay perfectly still, hoping that I won't say something I would regret later. My fingers tense up and I keep a super straight face.

Dad pulls up to a zebra crossing, and the traffic light burns bright red. He pulls out a box of mints from the inner door compartment. He prefers spearmint chewing gum, which is unfortunately banned in this city.

The real low-down is you can chew gum in Singapore but you can't buy it. If you decide to haul a box in from overseas, I suppose you would have to declare it for "personal use" to the customs dude if he decides to check your bags.

"You know, I really hate the old adage: Teenagers will be teenagers," Dad complains unexpectedly. "It's just so stereotypical."

I don't blink for five seconds straight.

"Why don't you ever talk to me? Why don't you ever share your feelings with me? Huh?"

This startles me quite a bit.

"I can never know what's on your mind, Dominic. Never."

Dad drives on and suspends the cross-examination. He should have been a prosecutor.

I want to defend myself, but all I can do is sigh. I press the "play" button on the car radio to find temporary solace.

Dad won't relent. He shoves my hand away, and says: "Are you for real? I can't believe you sometimes. Turn the radio off."

I'm officially out of options. Not that I dislike talking to Dad, but I don't feel especially right confiding in him about my most private of matters. Nor would I confide in my friends. Truthfully, I don't enjoy revealing the secrets of my life in front of anyone. It's way too embarrassing.

Fortunately, Dad receives a call from his golf buddy who is meeting us at the mall to have brunch at Toast Box. He lost his train of thought. Else, he realizes it's futile.

I stare blankly at the windshield, contemplating about what matters most right now. Reputation comes to mind first. Preserving my reputation is important. It's better this year as opposed to last year, but it could be better.

Hmm. On balance, I suppose I can be described as the following:

- Intelligent but not street-smart (MomTalk)
- Susceptible to peer pressure (cases in point: Talinda and Archie)
- Oft times weak, a clear pushover, succumbing to bullying, notably Ryan.
- Complacent, forgiving (Savannah)
- Reserved, unable to express my emotions (DadTalk).

My personality sort of matches Savannah's in that we are both introverted in our own ways. Savannah seems to seclude herself from schoolmates. I love talking to most schoolmates, but seldom my parents. This is wrong. This needs to change.

I suppose my hesitation to confess my struggles to Dad resides in the fear of being judged. I'm convinced that my parents' childhood—ahem, teenage years—pales in comparison to mine. Growing up in the 1970s must have been easier. Happy Days. All in the Family. The Brady Bunch. Good Times.

What's on tap these days? Narcos. Breaking Bad. Mad Men. The Vampire Diaries. Pretty Little Liars.

My mind wanders back to my first high school homeroom experience just a few days ago. Gosh. Why the heck did I instantly forgive Savannah? Now that I think of it, I actually should have been harsher on her. My clemency for her just proves my pushover-self.

That's who I am.

Without a doubt, Dominic's reprieve clears my mind for the upcoming year. Freshmen year is critical in terms of academics and extra-curricular activities.

For the first time, our transcripts will come into play as we make our way to our senior year. Any shortcomings in our transcript will have to be made up quickly as the academic studies will become ever more intense going forward.

Had Dominic not forgiven me for the YouTube incident, I don't think I would be able to concentrate in the slightest. My mind would just get convoluted.

For the first time in many years, I now look forward to my daily existence. Instead of finding fault with those around me or myself, I now tend to have a more outgoing personality.

Starting at home, I have been trying to engage more often with my sisters. Sister1 is preparing her final applications for college. Though she's a shoe-in for the universities that my parents attended, she's decided to strive for the Ivies and a few elite schools in the

Midwest and California. Sister2 may lead the cheerleading squad this year and now has branched out into Student Council.

Baby Sis and I are getting along quite well now. She's really come into her own in basketball, taking up the point guard position. Boys are invariably chasing her from time to time. Occasionally, Baby Sis would seek my advice when it comes to boys, although I will immediately deflect. My cynical view of boys is pretty much invalid.

Sister2 is far more naïve and gullible, but she would definitely be more expert at this topic.

Chapter 22
Rehash

Today is a different day. For some reason, I imagine my classmates are trying to ignore me. Word must have gotten around that Ryan Chang is continuing his campaign against me.

Inferiority is not a human feeling that can be described well. On the one hand, Ryan is not superior to me in any way. However, his mere presence somehow extinguishes everything in his path. It's a confounding existence.

Should I confront Ryan with equal ferocity, I am bound to secure a guaranteed seat in Sheriff Sadlowski's new digs. If I confide with a teacher or an administrator, I will garner the reputation of being a coward or a tattletale.

I have an occasional wingman in Archie but by no means do I have a troop. Nor would I ever enlist one.

"Wait, do you like Savannah? Are you going to ask her out?" the familiar voice follows me to the cafeteria during lunch. Archie's a human drone, the security version type that tracks one's every move in public space—except Archie complements the experience with sometimes aggressive, and always nonsensical banter.

I tense up quite a bit every time I ignore Archie's words.

"Huh? Can I get an answer?" he insists.

"What? Since when did this come about? No, I will not ask her out. I will never—ever—ask her out. When did you make that assumption?"

"Come on, man. Why? I saw the way you and Savannah conversed during lunch the other day. Too bad Triple Threat messed that up."

"You're kidding? You're imagining things again."

"I have a knack for sussing out what's going on."

"I know you can be overly creative."

"Are you in denial?" the pest continues.

I'm really frustrated now. The reckless banter has taken a toll. How was I so friendly to Archie all this while?

"No, are you? Because it really does seem as if you are. Don't you see, that girl, Savannah Dixon, was the hidden person who surreptitiously took that video?" I insist. "Why would I ever like her?"

"Whoa, Dominic, calm down, dude."

"Archie, you have messed with everything—and I mean everything has been messed up." The rigid index finger I am pointing at Archie is reminiscent of Mom's when I commit a bad deed, or when I forget the five mottos.

"Ever since the beginning, when you dared me to kiss Talinda. That's what started it all. If it weren't for you, I wouldn't have gotten into so much trouble, Savannah wouldn't have taken the video, and we wouldn't be standing here, arguing."

Silence continues for five long seconds. Fortunately, now we're sitting at the end of a long table that largely unoccupied. No one is within earshot.

Archie narrows his eyes, noting his incredulousness. "How dare you say that? Are you seriously blaming me for everything? It was ultimately your choice whether or not to kiss Talinda in the first place, not mine. Not to mention that you and Talinda decided where to meet up."

Wait a minute, that's true. I guess Archie has a point. It was ultimately my decision whether or not to kiss Talinda, even though I remember that I skeptically accepted the dare. Halfheartedly, but still executed.

In teenager-speak, dares are meant to be carried out. If you reject a dare, you're relegated to a lower status of coolness.

"Fine," I say, feeling awful. Flustered, I leave the cafeteria with my minestrone and ham sandwich. Archie's just officially won the argument, but I'm still mad at his bad influence on me over the months.

Peer pressure all pent up and now bent out of shape.

This is the crux of every teenage-driven argument. Best friends engage in verbal brawling. If one side voices an invalid argument, it's all over. And vice versa.

What's most frightening is that I still don't know if teenagers have short memories or otherwise. I'm guessing the latter, which makes me even more disgruntled.

But I know that Archie has an advantage from his point of view. He's got a far better reputation than I do.

While sipping fountain water next to the cafeteria, I notice Dominic and Archie quarreling. I don't need to hear a word to determine that Archie has the dominant hand.

Sometimes, boys who say little but strategically frown are wiser. That's Archie. He's winning this discussion, hands down.

For some odd reason, I fathom that they were speaking about me. I can't lip read but I have a sixth sense about this type of thing.

Dominic concedes by walking away from the fracas. Archie punctuates it with the inevitable face-palm, unnoticed by Dominic.

I'm witnessing everything from a vantage point where no one spots me. Immediately I subconsciously think of the day I videoed the kiss, as my mind veers off.

It's unfortunate as I thought Dominic had forgiven me about the horrid incident.

Dominic exits the cafeteria in a hurry, spilling minestrone on the ground with every step he takes. I want to approach him to console him. He bumps my shoulder impetuously with brute force nearly knocking me over. For three steps we continuously head in opposite directions, but when I hear his shoes screech to a complete stop, I stop as well.

I need to know what's on his mind.

Dominic shoots a rough glare at me for a few seconds, blinks furiously, and then stares down at the ground.

"I just want to make things clear. I shouldn't have forgiven you in the first place."

After he says this, I'm thinking he's going to walk away and leave me, but he is still there standing upright, delaying until I respond.

"Listen, I'm really sorry."

There's nothing more I can say. I wish I could find a possible synonym for "sorry" that would better fit the scenario. None comes to mind.

Dominic releases a sigh of disgruntlement as I'm left speechless. He's clearly showing no sign of forgiveness.

"Dominic," I call him back urgently, recapturing a bit of confidence.

Unfortunately, he is determined to move away, down the staircase. It's back to the status quo.

Chapter 23

One Last Chance—A Dreaded Witness

Savannah here.

School's out on a Friday afternoon. My watch reads "3:15 p.m."

It's odd how life deals me another blow. While other students happily make their way to departing buses or to the school driveway for pickup by their chauffeurs (either personal drivers or Moms), I tend to gravitate to the amphitheater after school.

I've got time.

The amphitheater is a common area for the entire Singapore International School campus. Though not an auditorium, it is a frequent staging ground for ad hoc events for primary school students up to high schoolers.

Semi-covered, the amphitheater is situated such that all schools radiate outward. After school, the area is usually deserted and quiet. I find it a refuge.

A few inches of rain are expected tomorrow, all too common for tropical Singapore. But for now, the weather seems to be overcast, without any rain.

I dislike gloomy days that don't offer any rain. It's humid, dreary and full of stuffiness. At least rain removes the pollution.

I'm standing next to my locker, where it's isolated. This is the place where I contemplate some of life's biggest questions.

Maybe I should see things a different way. Maybe I should place myself in Dominic's shoes, I think to myself.

How does Dominic truly perceive me? It's clear that he was premature in forgiving me that first day in homeroom.

Well, surely he sees me in a remarkably different way than I see myself. No doubt Dominic has reacted negatively over my latest intrusion, but what about before that?

I'm so unsure.

But Dominic probably doesn't know something from me. That I like him and I respect his character and genuineness. In any event, he would never know that. It's that I can't divulge all my secrets and that I have to keep all of them to myself: in my heart, in my brain, in my memory.

Forever cached.

Catharsis for me; mental block for Dominic.

I step up to the outermost part of the terrace, which overlooks the amphitheater. Subtle raindrops begin to fall on me as I walk further and further outwards, where there is no roof above. If I could run across the adjacent concrete footpath, I wouldn't feel any rain land on my back.

But I'm letting the rain freely fall on my back. My shirt absorbs each drop, one by one by one.

Out from the bottom of the amphitheater staircase, I suddenly see Dominic and the two wingmen forming Triple Threat. The gang is on the floor below me but I can see them clearly.

This is massive and foreboding. I wonder what's going on.

Suddenly, Ryan zooms out from behind the pillar. This is the final curtain call for Triple Threat.

As Dominic attempts to flee, Ryan and his menacing allies victimize him.

"Stop it, you guys!" Dominic yelps, trying to utilize some of the psychological techniques Ms. Steele, one of the school counselors, and the P.E. teachers, taught the students. In any bullying scenario, she noted that there are ways that victims can deal with bullies:

- *request assistance,*
- *assert yourself confidently but not stridently,*
- *use low-key humor but dispense with sarcasm, and*
- *own up to your situation.*

Obviously, Ryan and his affiliates attended the class too and devised a plan to outsmart it.

Help is not to be found as the school day is over and the entire school is making their way home on this Friday afternoon. There are no after-school activities on Fridays.

It's three against one and Dominic could easily be overpowered.

Any humor uttered by Dominic would only delay the inevitable. Sometimes, cracking a joke before a larger audience would buy some time for the victim. However, most often, joking around will backfire. And I don't see Mr. Sadlowski or any other person of authority nearing the scene anytime soon.

Owning up to the situation doesn't apply here. Dominic has undoubtedly expressed this thought for the past year or more. In any event, psychobabble like this won't help Dominic in any way.

Everyone knows these mainstream strategies. They don't help.

After a few more seconds, I grunt to myself and with great haste, I pull my iPhone out of my backpack. The ugly scene is about to unravel. It's another iteration of Dominic's lengthy battle with bullying.

This is the denouement. I close my eyes ever so tightly, hoping I won't mess up this time. And I vow that I won't ever regret this.

With my nimble digits, I quickly unlock my phone, readying it for what might transpire next.

At first, Ryan lunges over to Dominic, who appears to face what will be utter humiliation.

"Wasn't this the spot you kissed my sister?" Ryan asks contemptuously.

"Nope, actually, it was over there," Dominic tries some humor. It will fail.

"Yes. This was the spot. X marks the spot. Kiss it. Lick it," Ryan browbeats.

Kenny and Danny are just automatons, repeating Ryan's every word and gesticulating along the way.

Dominic doesn't deserve this much hatred over an event that happened over a year ago. Who knows if Ryan asked Talinda for her side of the story. I always surmised that the kiss was a dare by that kid Archie. I witnessed Talinda acting entirely game when Dominic moved forward for that peck on the lips.

"Kiss the ground? You're out of your mind!"

Unimpressed with Dominic's retort, Ryan thrusts his arms forward, knocking his victim to the floor.

Obviously planned, Ryan then screams: "Let's do it."

In an orchestrated move, the henchmen snatch Dominic's sneakers while Ryan pulls off Dominic's track pants.

"Please, stop it!" Dominic screams.

He now lies in a fetal position with his arms covering his boxer shorts. He looks around aimlessly, absolutely helpless.

That's not the end of it. Ryan summarily walks over to the ledge and tosses Dominic's track pants onto the gathering area for the departing buses below.

The Triple Threat then commences kicking.

I see it all.

The track pants land on the head of Hal Marks as he attempts to board his bus home. He does a double take and backs away from the bus. The other kids in line stumble over one another, as they laugh their heads off.

Hal thinks he's being pranked but he doesn't spot a victimizer so he calms down. His only worry is if someone caught it on video.

By this time, Archie, who's a few steps away, recognizes that the track pants belong to his buddy Dominic. He also heard Dominic scream out in protest a few seconds earlier.

For a moment, I see Sheriff Sadlowski, who's on bus duty. He realizes that something is amiss. Within seconds, he and several dozen students decide to vacate the staging area for the buses and make their way upstairs to the amphitheater.

Ryan spots Mr. Sadlowski and immediately relents, totally startled. Ryan recognizes that he has overstepped and summons Kenny and Danny to bolt. "Crap. Crew, we have to get outta here!"

All of a sudden, Kenny catches a glimpse of me.

"Wha—who is that?" Danny queries. "Who is that emo-looking chick?"

"It's Savannah Dixon, the YouTube girl," Kenny proclaims. "Oh no, was she recording us?"

"Bodacious18!" Danny exclaims. "Holy—she was recording us."

Uh-oh.

The first time Ryan peeks in my direction, he walks back two steps in astonishment. He then decides escaping the scene is far more important than worrying about someone videoing him.

"Guys, there's no time to fret over that," Ryan exclaims. "Sadlowski is on our case. Let's go!"

Dominic sees me and turns his head around. He's at a total loss as to how to react. "What are you doing up there?" he asks.

He doesn't get a response.

I sprint upstairs. I retreat.

What right does "Triple Threat" have to victimize me in such a way? I didn't do anything to them. I kissed Ryan's sister, but that's not a good enough reason to justify this incident.

Ryan doesn't seem to register the fact that Talinda was also entirely complicit. She "TBH'd" me, daring me to meet her in the amphitheater for that split-second kiss. I wonder if Ryan sought his sister's explanation of the entire situation.

Does that really matter whatsoever at this stage?

Frankly, had I known Talinda was Ryan's sister, I would have avoided her entirely.

And who do Kenny and Danny think they are? What right do new kids have to do such a thing? How could they have the wherewithal to jump into the midst? When Ryan let his emotions out on me, Kenny and Danny just nodded their heads repetitively. Sort of like Moby when he beeps his chest after Tim says something clever in

BrainPOP videos. But Moby never acted like a d*ck, ahem, jerk.

I swear, they're just "yes" men. It's so lame.

Within seconds, Sadlowski and a posse of students make their way to the amphitheater. Somehow, both Triple Threat and Savannah evade the scene without being spotted by the assistant principal.

"Dominic! Bro, are you okay?" Archie says. "Sorry I couldn't protect you. Who did this to you?" As if he were clueless. As if he could have stopped the bulldozer, as he had promised before.

Beaten down physically and psychologically, I can't offer a name, much less an explanation. At least not now. My only concern is to cover up. Quickly.

"Thank goodness you wore boxer shorts today, not your tighty whities," Riley chimes in. "I don't see any wedgie action."

Riley, please shut up, I think to myself.

"Noice. Are those Captain Underpants underwear?" Tammy Moody offers.

"Yet another YouTube spectacle in the making!" Jesse Ross declares. "Great way to start the new year! But wait, where's Savannah?"

"Here, I'll cover for you," Archie insists, trying to shield me a bit with his puny umbrella.

"You've said that so many times, Archie," I say, rolling my eyes.

Out of breath after tackling several flights of stairs, Hal Marks finally makes his way to this unforgettable scene, without my track pants. "Wow, did I miss something? This school is non-stop excitement."

Mr. Sadlowski quickly surveys the scene and realizes that the culprits of the infraction have disappeared. He then calls a teacher downstairs to hold all departing buses for 10 minutes.

"Alright, you kids, I need every one of you, except Dominic and Archie, to leave this area. You need to board your buses immediately. Hal, you can catch your breath for one minute before you retreat. You must need a breather."

"Nah, I'm good," he replies. "I'm walking downstairs this time around. But Mr. Sadlowski, I need to retrieve the track pants. I think they are Dominic's."

"Darn," Riley says. "This was just getting good."

"That's the breaks when Mr. Sadlowski is in charge," Jess grimaces.

Archie and I move toward the back of the amphitheater to regroup.

"Archie, thank you for helping Dominic today. You can catch your bus home if you leave now," Mr. Sadlowski says.

Archie's face exhibits his disapproval, as he'd like to support me further. He obliges, withdrawing from the scene.

"Now, Dominic, I will need to have a word with you in my office. We need to get to the bottom of this. In the meantime, I will see if one of the school counsellors is available. I will call your parents to see if they can pick you up later.

"You have been through an ordeal."

Speechless, I nod my head in agreement.

Chapter 24
Technology Fail

On this fateful day, once again I am relegated to witnessing another dramatic (and traumatic) school event.

Ryan and his Triple Threat cohorts commit one of the most egregious of bullying tactics. In high school, it should spell suspension. In college, they would call it hazing.

I witnessed the incident from the very same spot in which I witnessed Dominic and Talinda kiss. My natural reaction was to reach for my smartphone once again.

One of the Triple Threat members might have seen me from my vantage point, which compelled me to make a dash for the school library. I figured that I could catch the 4 o'clock departing buses after hiding in one of the library carrels.

Mrs. Lui, the ancient librarian, doesn't look up as I enter the library. She's engaged in assessing fines for late returned books.

I venture toward the back of the library where the old yearbooks and related paraphernalia are kept. No one hangs out back here.

I drop my backpack to the floor and pull out my smartphone.

I try to unlock the phone but the password prompt does not show up. The screen is resolute in blocking me.

"Shoot," I say under my breath. Could my iPhone be frozen? Panicked, I alternate between touching the screen and the Home button a few more times.

Of all days, why did my iPhone conk out today?

I have no other choice but to restart it by holding down the Home button and the Lock button for 10 long seconds.

The smartphone finally restarts.

I fast blink as I scan the media folders for the errant video. "Come on, come on. Please," I say.

Seconds later, I happen upon the latest video.

My entire body shudders as I realize that the video of the bullying incident was cut off prematurely.

What happened here? Did the iPhone just suddenly freeze? Or did I accidentally bump the record button during the ruckus? It did finally freeze but who knows what exactly happened.

The video is only five seconds in length. The only snippet I recorded was Dominic being surrounded by Triple Threat.

There's no evidence of Ryan haranguing Dominic to kiss the ground.

There's no evidence of Ryan shoving Dominic to the ground.

There's no evidence of Ryan's crew removing Dominic's sneakers while Ryan pulls off his track pants.

And there's no evidence that Ryan tossed Dominic's track pants over the ledge onto the bus staging area below.

My first instinct is to speak with Dominic to let him know that I witnessed the incident and would be fully backing him up in explaining the episode to the school administration.

That said, how could I admit that I have an incomplete video of the incident? Not to mention that I shouldn't have been in the amphitheater area Friday after school.

Never mind that I also resolved to myself that I would refrain from shooting videos of any one, not to mention that the victim is Dominic.

Looking back, I would think that Dominic would be irritated by my actions. When he called out to me prior to Mr. Sadlowski's arrival to the scene, I didn't respond and instead, dashed away to catch my bus.

Dominic may be fearful that I would automatically upload a second hardcore video onto YouTube. It doesn't matter that I only possess an incomplete video of the scene.

Neither my parents nor my elder sisters would be viable options either. My parents would probably shake their heads and take the entire matter in their own hands. Don't forget that neither the school nor my parents punished me for uploading the original video on YouTube.

Now is not the time to confide in them.

My elder sisters would probably ask me to communicate with Dominic and pass him the incomplete video. I'm not sure whether I should implicate myself in this fashion.

It's hard to fathom how just a short time ago, I was bullied by my worst enemy and his alter egos. I did sense that Ryan was going to instigate another bullying session after that recent encounter in the lunchroom.

The thing is, Ryan's main mission in life is to bully others—it's second nature to him. As I've mentioned earlier, he doesn't have a proper reason for doing so. It's like he's in the primary school playground.

"*Res ipsa loquitur.*"

This is a legal term that Grandpa quoted a lot when he was a lawyer. It means that the crime speaks for itself.

Let's put this incident into perspective.

Kenny told me after lunch that he wanted me to consider joining the rugby team. Having tried out successfully for the junior varsity team, he asked me to meet him and a couple of other players in the amphitheater after school. The thrust of the discussion was to find out how he and his teammates could expedite my joining the team, despite my inexperience in the sport.

I should have known better. Naïve me blanked out on the fact that Kenny is a new kid.

Ryan and his crew cornered me in the amphitheater and gave me a shellacking that I will never forget. By this time, no fewer than half of the school will be knowledgeable as rumors of this nature spread like bacteria.

It's not a rumor, in fact. Three classmates humiliated me. And several dozen classmates saw me disheveled in my boxer shorts, lying in a fetal position on the floor of the amphitheater.

No video is required.

I should have planked or done something hilarious. Unfortunately, I was in no mood for anything like that.

Assistant Principal Sadlowski seemed sympathetic but for the fact that I was discovered in the same venue that caused so much misery in the past year. Why couldn't this have occurred anywhere else in the entire school?

And what's up with Savannah?

Was she stalking me? Why does she always appear during the troughs of my young life?

Kenny mentioned that she was in the environs. Did she have her iPhone at the ready?

Did she record the dubious deed? Worse yet, will she upload it onto YouTube? Stomp, the Singapore cousin of YouTube, would be another option. Better yet, why not upload on both websites?

That night, Mom and Dad had a major chat with me—the first serious huddle since the Talinda incident. It was almost like an intervention.

Mom was quite distraught to receive the call from Mr. Sadlowski, who described the episode afterschool. She quickly called Dad to discuss what happened.

Mom picked me up from school after I had a short meeting with Mr. Sadlowski, providing him with the details of the event. He said that he would also contact the parents of the "alleged" culprits.

"Son, what happened?" Mom exclaimed as I opened the passenger car door. Erin was in the back seat.

"Dominic, are you alright?" Erin asked.

"It was an ugly scene, Mom," I explained. "Ryan Chang and a couple of other boys confronted me in the amphitheater."

"For goodness sake, why were you in that area after school? You know that's a no-go area."

"Mom, I was duped by one of Ryan's buddies. This kid, Kenny, a member of the junior varsity rugby team invited me to have a chat with him and a couple of other teammates. I'm not sure but I think one of them was impressed with my performance in gym class.

"It was a set-up, as Ryan and another kid were in waiting to surround me."

"That's crazy," Mom says. "I'm calling the police."

"Mom, it's not a police matter," Erin insists.

Chapter 25

Reputations Precede Us

"Mr. Sadlowski?" I peek inside the humongous conference room. I'm standing at the doorway, and immediately I notice Ryan, Kenny and Danny perched upright on their seats. Ryan's never looked so remorseful.

I have no reference point for the newbies.

Ryan's face is sullen and dark as the brooding clouds outside. Kenny and Danny are an odd sight. They stare at each other's shoelaces.

It's Monday afternoon after school, three days following the incident.

I barge into the hearing—uninvited, unannounced. For some reason, I don't feel any vindication, only apprehension.

In spite of my intrusion, Dominic faces the other direction. He doesn't turn around to acknowledge me. I wonder what he's thinking.

No fewer than five—perhaps more—sets of parents are seated around the room, joined by a few other school administrators and counsellors. My dear parents soon follow suit, gently knocking on the door and entering unprompted.

"Please take a seat," Mr. Sadlowski says to me and my parents.

"The basis of this meeting is that it is alleged that three students engaged in bullying a student in the amphitheater area of the school," Mr. Sadlowski continues. "I understand that we have a witness to the events that took place. That witness is Savannah Dixon. Savannah, do you have any introductory words?"

"Have these three fellows fully explained their involvement?" I ask.

"No, they haven't," declares Ms. Grace Sullivan, the head principal. "In fact, although they admit they were in the environs, they claim that they did not remove Dominic's track pants and launch them over the ledge."

Ms. Sullivan also hints at her lack of patience in the matter.

"Young lady, do you have something you would like to contribute?"

I nod.

"Well, I guess we have to do it the hard way, then," I say. Composed, I pull out my phone and grasp it in front of me.

For some reason, I make the move ever so methodically so as to treasure the moment. I purposely mistype my password to terrorize Ryan.

The combined expressions on the three culprits are just absolutely brilliant.

Ryan's jaw hits the floor. He stops blinking. His mother, perhaps more knowledgeable about my reputation as a YouTuber, double face-palms. For an adult, this is grabbing your face. Mr.

Chang, his father, clenches his teeth, then his fists, wondering what's my next move.

Talinda is not present. This really doesn't involve her in any way.

Kenny drops his head even lower, such that his hippie hair now covers his entire face. His mother, who was sitting somewhat upright, now slouches in despair. His father tries to comfort her by embracing her with his right arm.

Danny and his parents simultaneously cock their heads sideways and stare out into empty space. Pity they do not have additional kids in attendance.

Dominic, by the way, finally turns around to face me. I imagine he tries to wink at me but the less dominant eyelids do not actually touch. Good enough. His parents' eyes light up in anticipation.

I can't see my parents as they took a seat in the back.

Ryan knows in his mind that I have a video in my phone of the incident, and if he fails to confess the real truth, I will present the video to Ms. Sullivan and Mr. Sadlowski as hard evidence of another major school infraction, shutting him down.

I yield to the above-mentioned principles and hold my ground. Five seconds pass. I slow my breathing down considerably and hold back.

"Ms. Sullivan, Mr. Sadlowski—I have something very serious I have to confess," Ryan reluctantly murmurs as he clenches his fist

tightly. He actually conjures up the nerve to speak up. I stop what I am doing.

That's a real brave move, so he deems as his only choice.

Somehow if he confesses, Ryan believes that he will receive a lighter punishment. The ignominy associated with the episode might be lessened if the confession precedes the viewing of the video.

Quite the opposite.

Oft-times inaction is better than action. For some actions, there are sometimes movements sideways.

In Ryan's case, the threat of extinction prevails over common sense. Remaining silent would have been a better choice. He has not read the Fifth Amendment right against self-incrimination.

The Fifth Amendment doesn't apply in tropical Singapore, nor does it help students in peril.

Ryan looks at Kenny and Danny, then says: "We were all involved in bullying Dominic. All of us. I was the ringleader.

"It was all me. I asked Kenny to invite Dominic on false pretenses to talk about joining the junior varsity rugby team. That discussion took place at the amphitheater.

"Before meeting after school, I strategized with Kenny and Danny. We verbally harassed Dominic and forced him to kiss the ground where he kissed my sister last year.

"Failing that, I shoved Dominic to the ground. Once on the ground, Kenny and Danny ripped off his sneakers while I pulled off his pants.

"Honestly, it was just a prank.

"I am so sorry for the bullying incident. It will never happen again."

Well, it won't happen again, I think to myself. At least not at this school.

Kenny and Danny look at each other and chime in: "We are sorry and it will never happen again."

This is a clear example of public shame, utter disgrace. In my case, pregnant pauses are the some of the best things in life.

Yup. Ryan should have abstained from confessing until the video was presented.

Mr. Sadlowski raises one eyebrow, then confirms my initial thought. "Well, it won't happen again, Ryan. And here's why. I'm really not surprised, Mr. Ryan Chang, of your reckless behavior. I can't even count the number of times you've been involved in bullying. It's as if that's the only thing in which you excel."

Ms. Sullivan grimaces at Mr. Sadlowski's last comment.

"I can only echo the sentiment of Mr. Sadlowski, who is all too familiar with the shenanigans of Mr. Ryan Chang. As I understand, this is the culmination of several incidents through the course of his Middle School years," Ms. Sullivan interjects. She needs to take charge.

"As for you other two young men, I am shocked that you would endanger your otherwise solid reputations to join Mr. Chang in this escapade. You guys are new students but this is unforgivable. Kenny,

I will have a word with Coach Bradley on your improper representation of the JV rugby team.

"Danny, I am certain this breach of the Student Code will result in dire consequences for you as well."

Ryan now looks pitiful. He glances back at Dominic, then directly at me and then, my phone. He is now desperate.

"Well, are you going to show Mr. Sadlowski the video?" Ryan says, somewhat sarcastically. He kind of has nothing to lose.

"Yes. I will." I cautiously step up to the Assistant Principal's desk and hand him my iPhone.

"Triple Threat" cringes in pain. Dominic appears somewhat uneasy as well. He will have to relive the experience for the world to see.

"Just make sure he doesn't project the video on the big screen," Dominic whispers to me.

"No. You don't get it. Check this," I say to him. This is the most crucial part of this plan.

"The video is incomplete," I assert.

Silence.

Dominic is relieved, and in mild shock. He won't face further scrutiny by the audience. Boxer shorts are all too personal. "Actually?" he says.

"Actually," I reply. "You'll see."

Mr. Sadlowski scrambles to screen the video via the iPhone and Apple TV onto a projection screen.

The video only shows the Triple Threat congregating in the amphitheater with Dominic in tow. No verbal harassment, no shoving, no disrobing, no pants tossing recorded.

Immediately, Ryan's face lights up. "Wait—does that mean I'm let off? There's no evidence here. Guys, we're good to go," he proclaims.

Kenny and Danny suddenly perk up and stand up.

"No," Mr. Sadlowski declares. "You stay here." For once, he recognizes the true gravity of the proceedings. Incidentally, he doesn't try to make a joke that falls flat.

Yes. I know exactly where we are going with this. My plan works out.

Empowered not with a full video of the bullying episode, but with a reputation of being a YouTube videographer, I testify—without really saying anything—that I was witness to the event. What Dominic felt and sensed in the incident, I was a direct eyewitness. No video is necessary.

Memories cached, forever etched in my mind. But yet, I need to say nothing more.

"The fact that you voluntarily confessed to this recent bullying session with Dominic is equal or superior to a video shot from afar. Need I say more?" Mr. Sadlowski suggests.

"In fact," Ms. Sullivan continues, "Savannah's presence as a witness further confirms Dominic's rendition of what actually transpired. It's now not only his word against the word of the hooligans, excuse me, the trio of culprits."

Ryan glances at his cohorts. He clenches both of his fists even tighter and locks his knees. "Shoot," he mumbles under his breath.

I've tamed Ryan. He has been conned into my trap. I don't know of anyone who's done that before.

In some ways, I directly caused his predicament by keeping my secret to myself. Had I divulged to Dominic before the proceedings, for example, that I had an incomplete video, he might have wavered in standing up against Ryan and his henchmen.

Even Sadlowski was inexplicably easy on Ryan through the years despite his numerous transgressions.

"Do you ever wonder why you're still here in this school, despite all the nuisance you've caused to people your age, or worse, younger than you?" Sadlowski says.

I don't know exactly where Mr. Sadlowski's going with this, but I have a feeling that the unsuspecting Ryan will succumb to this lecture one last time. He's going to get expelled.

"Every time after you were involved in a troublemaking situation, you, your parents and I would meet to forge a detailed

plan to prevent you for doing such horrible things again. All of the school counsellors tried their best to assist but all of this was in vain. In so many ways, we all failed.

"We queried whether you bully to seek personal joy, or because of a deeper, more diabolical, reason."

Dominic appears calm. Ryan's parents further grimace. Dominic's mother is beaming.

"So," Mr. Sadlowski continues. "Let me push you further on this question because this is important.

"Do you bully people out of pleasure?"

This is a ridiculously pressing question for Ryan, who's contemplating a wise-guy answer. That probably won't play well. Not now, not ever again.

"Ryan?"

"Well, now that you brought that up, I think I do. I mean, I've never thought about it that way."

"Let's put it in another perspective. Do you bully people for any specified reason?"

"Well, no . . ."

"Then why did you choose to bully me just now?" Dominic barges in, having remained mute this whole time.

Ryan stifles a sigh, holding his breath half-way. "I don't know why I had to bully you last Friday. Well, you did kiss my . . ."

"Let me stop you right there, young man," Mr. Sadlowski interjects. "You have absolutely no basis to use that as an excuse to

bully Dominic. Even if Dominic had known you had a sister—he tells me that he did not—that is no basis for your egregious behavior."

Mr. Sadlowski is finally standing up for Dominic! And Ryan is getting wrecked.

"Additionally, I am aware of numerous occasions in which you bullied Dominic. Once in the men's changing room, a second time in the lunchroom and now this latest episode. In addition to that, you, Mr. Chang, are responsible for bullying many other people."

Ryan has absolutely zero evidence to defend himself. This line of questioning only delays the inevitable.

"We need to discuss this further," Ms. Sullivan informs the group and taps Mr. Sadlowski's shoulder, signaling him to go outside. "There will be an official statement in a few minutes."

Ms. Sullivan now takes the podium.

"Mr. and Mrs. Chang, I regret to inform you that your son, Ryan Chang will be expelled from Singapore International School as of today. His three incidents of bullying involving just Dominic—standing alone—is sufficient to expel him in accordance with the Student Handbook. I understand that Mr. Sadlowski's file contains other incidents against other students as well.

"This decision is final. Mr. and Mrs. Chang, should you and Ryan seek to appeal this decision, you will have to make an application with the Board of Supervisors.

"Based upon what I have heard in this hearing and my review of Mr. Ryan Chang's file, I am quite certain that my decision will be backed up by our Board of Supervisors. I trust that you will not lodge an appeal lightly."

Pause.

"Meeting adjourned," Mr. Sadlowski proclaims.

"You are dismissed," Ms. Sullivan declares.

Now I finally realize Savannah is a godsend, albeit a sleeper. Had she not again hovered above the amphitheater last Friday, I would be facing another predicament: Ryan and his crew bullying me, compounded by the ever-complacent assistant principal.

She was actually smart in holding back on informing those around her that her iPhone froze at the start of the video. I suppose she was flabbergasted by the quick downward spiral turn of events caused by Ryan.

I know I was.

Barging into the student disciplinary hearing, Savannah purposefully gave all those in attendance the stark impression that once again, she videoed a major school event. Her reputation preceded her.

Duped, Ryan spoke too soon to confess the entire details of the ugly saga. He not only implicated himself but also his doting followers.

What a brutal mistake.

What was even more brutal were Ms. Sullivan's words declaring Ryan's inevitable expulsion.

Ryan well deserved the punishment exacted. Honestly, it should've happened a long time ago.

Truth is, he should have been expelled last year after his horrendous pranks in the weeklong excursion in Chiang Mai.

I don't know why I didn't speak out.

In fact, no one who witnessed the flamethrower in action said a single word about it after returning to school. No doubt Millennials are desensitized due to the Net, video games, movies, cable TV and mass media in general.

Ryan Chang.

What a hoodlum.

As the attendees to the proceeding leave the conference room, Ms. Sullivan reprimands Mr. Sadlowski. We eavesdrop.

"Grace, I'm so glad I'm done with this Ryan Chang kid. I mean, it's been six long years handling this troublemaker. I can't go on ear-dragging for much longer!" Mr. Sadlowski remarks. "I've had a long day. I'll see you in the morning."

"Well, not so fast, Samuel, I'm not done here," Ms. Sullivan retorts. "You and I need to have a chat with the Board of Supervisors. I am not convinced that you have acted in accordance with the school administration policies with respect to this matter."

For the first time, Mr. Sadlowski's countenance exudes fear. "Wait, what?" he says, pretending he's done nothing wrong.

I don't care to eavesdrop on their conversation. I can already predict Mr. Sadlowski's fate.

How in the world was Sadlowski promoted from being the assistant principal of middle school to that same position in the high school? Truthfully, he's unfit for the job. Thanks to Sadlowski, Ryan has been running rampant all these years despite his appalling behavior.

At least Mr. Sadlowski stood up for me for once. Given the circumstances, that's all I care about.

My parents are also a bit shaken from the meeting as well. They can't seem to fathom how a boy like me would succumb to Ryan and his henchmen.

"How could you let these three bully you like that? That never happened to me," Mom recalls. "When I was your age, I was one tough mama. I swear.

"The only time I was terrorized was when one of my classmates deliberately cut some of my hair off in Primary 3. My teacher forced that naughty girl to stuff my hair into an envelope, seal it and send it back home for her mother to sign."

"You never told me about that episode before," I remark.

"Yep, I was in quite an unfortunate situation as I was regarded as the only near-bald girl in the school. Anyways, see you at home. I assume you're going to take the 4:00 bus, right?" Mom puts her hand on my shoulder.

"Yes, I'll take the 4:00 bus," I reply.

"I will get the car and drop Mom at home, but I need to go back to work first," Dad says as he takes a sip of water at the water fountain. "In that case, I'll catch you later. See you."

Mom gives me a hug like no other while my Dad offers a fist bump.

Dad probably has stories to tell but for once, he is not sharing. Perhaps he did not want to compound an already humiliating and dreadful situation. In any event, he had something else on his mind—the office.

Either way, I'm appreciative.

My parents head off and I swing by the lockers to retrieve my backpack. As I head towards the staircase, I see Savannah already all the way down, about to open the main entrance doors. This time, her eyes aren't trained on her iPhone.

"Hey," I begin, smiling at her, catching up to her.

"Hey there," she replies, politely holding the door for me. We make our way toward the bus staging area. Side-by-side.

Savannah exhales a deep breath after several seconds of complete silence between the two of us. "You know, I still don't understand why you had to be so mean to me the other day. Are you still holding grudge for what I did?"

Before I answer, a sweaty Archie jogs up to us. He had just finished football practice. "Hey, Big Dom, what's up? How did the session with the higher-ups go? Did Ryan get bounced outta here? Oh, hi, Savannah."

"Not a good time, man. Can I catch you later? I'll Skype you later," I say.

"Oh." Winking as best he can, Archie bids his farewell and bails from the photo-bomb opp. "Sure thing. Don't do anything I wouldn't do," he whispers to me.

Savannah and I stop for a second while I try to come up with an answer to her question.

"No, Savannah. Actually, that had nothing to do with you. I was just over-reacting to the entire situation. Your apology was readily given and I should have held true to my word. I forgave you the first time."

"Really?"

"Yes. We're all good." I smile.

We both continue to the buses. Odd how teens treasure silence over chit-chat.

"What Ryan and his gang did to you was really, really atrocious. What was that?" Savannah restarts the conversation.

"I really have no clue. Bullies like Ryan choose their victims when they least expect it. All I really care about now is that he's expelled. Gone. The kid really got clobbered," I laugh a bit.

"No kidding, he got what he deserved. He really dished out a lot of pain over the years. He and his parents will need to find another school," Savannah says.

"Yep, and that's no easy task. There are so many expatriate families moving to Singapore and local kids who want in. Every school has a waitlist and won't be receptive to Ryan's track record. And man, where's Ryan going to go? Let's not discuss Talinda—ha, I'm over her," I reply.

"And don't forget about Sheriff Sadlowski. He also got hammered," Savannah laughs.

"Yeah, two for the price of one."

"Good one."

Just before we head onto our buses, I need to make sure Savannah hears my appreciation. "Savannah, I mean what you did last Friday was really gutsy. It was bold. I'll have to admit, I got kind of intimidated when I saw you up there, videoing me. I thought it was going to be a repeat of last year."

"Really?" Savannah squints her eyes ever so slightly.

"I hope it's not a YouTube special. If it is, I will find it, and I will flag it," I joke. "I will shut you down."

Savannah chuckles. "No, no. I just had to do something to defend you. I'm on your side. Don't worry, I didn't get any footage of you in your boxer shorts. Trust me."

"Hey, Savannah, can I ask you something?" I ask.

"Sure, anything."

"Did your iPhone really freeze or did you purposely stop the video recording?"

She pauses.

"I'll let you decide," she says, winking one eye.